Kiss of Scandal

Isabel Roman

Kiss of Scandal

Ravenous Romance™
100 Cummings Center
Suite 123A
Beverly, MA 01915

ISBN-13: 978-1-60777-630-7

This book is a work of fiction, and any resemblance to persons living or dead is purely coincidental.

Dedication

To my dear friend from Texas, Raelyn. All this is her fault. To Christine and Jeannette, you know why. Special thanks to Evangeline Holland for the map.

Chapter One

St. Petersburg, Russia
February 5, 1855
Georgian Calendar

Bastard.

COUNT PETER Andreiovitch Orlov pounded his silver-tipped walking stick on the roof of the carriage. His heart pounded in time to the quick clatter of the horses' hooves, which moved too slowly.

"Faster!" he bellowed to the driver. Gusts of wind and snow howled around the carriage, impeding their rapid movement.

His hand drifted to the case on the seat beside him, checking once again that his proof lay safe. He'd long suspected something these past years, perhaps a bit of smuggling or tidbits of information passed to the enemy. But nothing as deep-rooted as he'd found.

The tsar will crush his family.

The metal sled suspending the carriage tore through the heavy snow blanketing the streets. Jerking the curtain back to check their progress, Peter stared past the frost as the glowing lampposts blinked by. At this speed, they should reach the Winter Palace within minutes.

With impatient fingers, he opened his pocket watch and noticed it was almost two in the morning. There'd be a delay in waking the tsar, and the attendants would try to block his visit. Hell, they'd commit murder before waking the emperor.

Tapping the case once again, though it could not have disappeared, Peter nodded to himself. "He has to know *now*."

Leaning forward, as if by sheer will he could move the carriage faster, Peter thought of his family and the politics of this untenable situation. The tsar's temper would flare uncontrollably, but they'd have to consider the nobility. This must be handled with utmost caution.

Peter's head jerked up; he'd heard a distinctive sound through the howl. *A pistol shot.* Wiping the fog off the window, he peered out once more.

The carriage veered sharply to the right, away from the Palace route. "Driver!" he yelled. "Stay on course!"

Looking out the window, he saw two other horses, each with a rider, racing alongside the carriage. His driver screamed something he couldn't make out as the carriage rocked violently from the sharp turn.

Opening his case, Peter removed several of the more important papers: detailed expenses, a travel itinerary, and a small leather book listing accounts. Without a second thought, he knelt on the floor and separated the seat from its frame with a hard yank. Stuffing the papers into the hollow gap, he pushed it back. Sitting down again and bracing his feet on the opposite bench for more leverage, Peter pushed the edge with his walking stick, wedging the frame into place. Glancing around the interior to make sure nothing was amiss, he snapped the lid of his case shut.

Peter pulled out his revolver. With the erratic rocking of the carriage slowing, he opened the door just in time to see one of the riders throw something at his driver. He tried to block the onslaught of snow hitting his face with his left hand, and leaned his shoulder against the door frame to steady himself.

Over the howl of the winter storm, the horses cried and the carriage came to a jolting stop. Peter jumped from the velvet interior into the whipping snow, gun held high before him. With a steady pace, he approached the rider he could see. There had been two, but he dared not look for the second man.

"Who are you?" he demanded. "Dismount immediately!"

The man jumped off his horse, face covered with heavy winter garb. Peter noticed, in the dim light from the lamppost, that he was dressed as a gentleman.

"I was trying to help," the rider screamed through the biting wind. "You were about to race into an overturned carriage. There is an accident down Nevsky Prospekt, near the Palace."

"Where's my driver?" Peter kept the revolver aimed squarely at the stranger's chest.

Looking around as if the driver lay buried in the snow bank, the man gestured for Peter to lower his weapon. "He must have dismounted from the other side." The stranger pointed. "There, behind you— your driver."

Keeping aim on the stranger, Peter turned his head and was met with a strike to the temple. He collapsed, but didn't lose consciousness. He felt groggy, as if struggling to wake from a dream. Blinking, he searched for his pistol, his bleary eyes focusing enough to see someone snatch it from the cushions of snow.

"Don't leave any blood on the ground," he heard one of them yell as they picked him up to move him back into the carriage.

Once inside the velvet box, the relative warmth seeped into his bones and he struggled to clear his head. Instinct told him this was no simple robbery. Without the screeching wind drowning everything out, he found he could hear them more clearly.

"Get the papers from the case. Hurry."

Peter tried to move but found he'd lost control of his limbs. Pain spiked through him, momentarily blinding him as he struggled not to moan aloud.

"Give me those and take these," the stranger commanded. *That voice*, Peter thought as his vision cleared. He knew that damn voice.

"Good. Done." One of the men opened the door. "Finish it."

The last thing Count Peter Andreiovitch Orlov saw was the metal base of the carriage's light fixture before he felt it crash against his head.

****

February 6, 1855
Georgian Calendar
The Winter Palace—St. Petersburg, Russia

A summer's day, Countess Katria Viktorevna Markova thought.

The Palace reminded her of a brilliant summer's day every time she entered. No matter that it was winter in Russia. Even with her velvet gown and sable cloak, she could barely stand the bitter winds that whipped through the air as she stepped from her carriage to the interior. Inside these walls, exotic plants flourished and the gilded accents sparkled like the sun at their summer villa on the Black Sea.

The beauty of the Palace served as a stark contrast to many who wandered her halls. The tsar's royal court gathered here for their daily rituals, peacocks prancing about and scheming with every breath. They were up there, strolling the Palace's state rooms. She could practically hear their venomous tongues working on whatever soul was the latest to fall into disfavor.

"Your Grace!" Katria called as she handed her cloak with a smile and a nod to a scarlet-liveried servant. Spotting her uncle about to ascend the ornate rococo staircase, she moved forward toward Bishop Anatoli Mikhailivitch Markova. His dark eyes watched her, his hand absently smoothing his long, impeccably trimmed beard. The medallion atop his black robes glittered like the gilded accents along the Palace walls.

"Good, you've arrived. I've been watching for you." Anatoli waved the hovering servant away with an imperious hand.

Katria started to bow from the waist, her right hand extending downward. She prepared to continue with the ritual when Anatoli laughed. "Shall we dispense with pretense?" He took her elbow, straightening her, and offered a welcoming embrace.

"Uncle, there never has and never will be pretense between us." Kissing him on both cheeks, Katria smoothed down his long, prickly beard before glancing curiously up the staircase. She could hear muffled voices floating down from the state rooms, and anticipation quickened through her blood.

"Are the vipers biting today or just snapping?" Her wry comment caused Anatoli's grin to widen.

She'd referred to the courtiers as vipers since she was a child; it was an apt description of more than half of them. But they were not the reason she wished to hurry to the rooms. Nor was the tempting array of food and drink, nor even the chance to interact with the tsar.

"I expect venom to spew forth momentarily," a deep voice rumbled from behind her.

She could feel his hot breath tickling her shoulder, skin tingling with awareness. His lips brushed the base of her neck, there and gone in a heartbeat. Scandalous in so public a setting. Heart racing, she forced herself to turn slowly, arching an eyebrow as Count Nikolai Andreiovitch Orlov joined her and Anatoli in front of the Jordan Staircase.

Her need to rush up to the state rooms vanished.

Drinking in his appearance, Katria kicked the hem of her heavy skirt as she faced him. Her focus left his eyes to slide down his tall, muscular frame. As tall as Anatoli, Nikolai towered over her. It was the look, however, the one she now knew he reserved for her, that inspired sinful thoughts whenever they met. She smiled.

"Count Orlov." She extended her hand, but instead of delicately kissing the back of it, Nikolai raised his dark eyes to meet hers and kissed her gloved palm. Katria tilted her head and offered a cordial nod for the benefit of any who may be watching.

"Countess." Nikolai offered his arm and they started up the stairs behind Anatoli. He closed his other hand over hers, keeping her close by his side. Katria couldn't say she minded. "The vipers are restless, slithering about the rooms in search of prey."

The way he'd said *"prey,"* the hungry look he slanted in her direction, made her shiver. Her fingers tightened on his arm, and Katria was certain he noticed. Then again, everything about Nikolai elicited reaction, from the strength of his arm to the power in his smooth, deep voice. Now, as they climbed the stairs, his fingers brushed over her wrist, teasing the bare inch of skin between glove and dress.

"I've missed you," Nikolai said. The words were so low, for a moment she wasn't certain she'd heard them. Then he chuckled, and the sultry sound went straight through her.

Katria shook her head, temporarily clearing her thoughts. *What* had they been talking about? Court, yes. Unsure why she'd shared it with him in the first place, she noticed he'd taken to her vipers metaphor. Only a handful knew of her habit of denigrating the tsar's court. It wasn't something she often shared, too used to hiding her true opinions.

"Father was called to a special meeting this morning, and I've come out of curiosity," Katria whispered as she paused on the stairs for a better hold of her skirt.

"I've heard there was an upset this morning. Before you ask, I am not privy to the details as yet," Anatoli offered. His strong voice, which usually reverberated along the huge Palace rooms, was hushed now so as not to be overheard as they continued to ascend the marble steps. The cavernous stairs could carry a voice to the very top, and none of them wished to have their conversation heard.

"You will be," she said with a quick grin up at him. Anatoli was one of the few people she believed in. She'd long wished he was her father instead of Viktor.

"You give me entirely too much credit, Katria."

"I doubt that, Your Grace," Nikolai said. But Katria noticed his gaze shifted to her, and offered a slight smile.

Each time their eyes met, she felt he wanted to possess her, devour her. At first, unbalanced by his attentions, his aggressiveness, she'd challenged him. Life at the royal court had taught her a great deal. Russian court was the most vicious arena, and she'd sworn at a very young age that she wouldn't be eaten alive. She'd find a way to bite back.

"That isn't possible, Uncle," she agreed. Pausing as they reached the top step, Katria peered across the landing through the opened archway, familiar with the court scene. Politics breathed life into Russian society.

"What intrigue is rattling the nest here today?" she asked, looking between the two men. Arm still secure through Nikolai's, she was grateful Anatoli was with them. Though part of her had grown to crave time alone with Nikolai, another part of her recognized his possessive need and bristled.

"Several, including a plot against General Khrulev which disturbs me greatly." Anatoli's voice hardened. "He's the only hope we have in this tangled mess of a war."

"He's one of our few competent generals." Nikolai's dry words were all too true.

"Who's spreading these plots? Radoff? Ulensky?" Katria removed her hand from Nikolai's arm to walk a few steps in front of him. "Those two see Khrulev in the way of their own military ambitions."

"Among others," Nikolai added with a hint of annoyance in his voice.

Katria stilled, looking back at Nikolai. Was that annoyance because of the latest plot? Or because she'd stepped away from him? She tried to discern the reason by watching him out of the corner of her eye, but couldn't tell.

A master of court life, Nikolai let nothing show he did not wish to. With her own private smile, she chose to believe he was annoyed that she moved away. There was a certain power in commanding such attention. Power that she rather enjoyed. She'd need to cultivate the way she used it. Especially since he had managed to best her at the most important turn in their game.

"Perhaps we can divert attention away from the general for a time?" Smiling back at her companions, Katria caught Nikolai's eye.

His smile changed: no more the playful political one, but one she couldn't describe. Deeper; inviting, even. She could see the look in his dark gaze follow her, feel it from a distance. She would never admit he could unnerve her. Never.

"We are of the same mind, Katria." Anatoli pushed his robe to one side to pace out of view of the open archway.

Anatoli was an imposing sight when his thick eyebrows furrowed. Katria, forcing her gaze from Nikolai to blindly watch her uncle pace, believed the tsar was slightly intimidated by her uncle's six-foot-tall, stocky frame. The thought always amused her.

"What shall we feed to those ravenous snakes?" Anatoli asked.

"I think you know, Uncle, and are wondering if I do as well." Katria shot him a sly gaze, one she would have prolonged had she not felt the urgent need to remove her jacket. She'd been chilled to the bone traveling the short distance from her home to here. How the tsar managed to keep this enormous Palace as warm as it was mystified her.

"The tsar's council of ministers. Galensky is finally going to relinquish his seat due to poor health." Returning her attention to Nikolai, she saw her statement invoked the half-smile, half-smirk she'd grown to recognize when something pleased him.

"I'm impressed, Katria. How did you discover this so quickly?" Anatoli's approving smile widened as he approached her.

"By way of maid and tailor. You've instructed me well, Uncle," she shot back in a conspiratorial tone.

Nikolai studied her. Over the last months, she'd often caught him watching her. No, not watching. Admiring. A surge of heat coursed through her.

It had become an obsessive diversion between them, this watching. This studying. She'd become keenly aware of it over the past months, of their own private chess match.

"You'll need every bit of skill for the future." The bishop's dark eyes turned serious. "When I leave this world, I want to be secure in the knowledge you are well prepared to navigate these rooms."

Warmth filled her at his words. Her uncle didn't often say such things or express much emotion. When he did, her affection deepened for the bishop, as did the resentment she held toward her father. The look in Anatoli's eyes said what he could not say aloud, and Katria smiled up at him.

"If you'll both excuse me." Nikolai's smooth voice brought her back to the moment. "I believe it's time the others learned of Galensky." Taking her by the shoulders, Nikolai kissed her temple. "Don't go far," he whispered. "Your Grace." He nodded before heading across the hall and through the archway.

"He is just the man to divert attention from Khrulev to Galensky," Anatoli said as Nikolai disappeared into the crowd. She could still feel his lips on her temple, but refused to touch the area he'd kissed. "We spoke about it just before you arrived."

Then her uncle paused to stare at her. Katria raised an inquiring eyebrow and maintained eye contact with him, though she wanted to track Nikolai's movements. Anatoli shook his head and sighed reprovingly. "It is written clearly on your face, my dear."

"What is?" Smoothing her bodice, Katria tilted her head toward the open state room, unable to resist following with her gaze Nikolai's tall form through the crowd.

"The love you have for your Nikolai. Every one of your features becomes radiant when his name is mentioned. When you are together it is painfully obvious."

Startled, Katria swung her gaze to her uncle. Love? Is that what he saw? Did she love Nikolai? Fascinated by him, yes, she felt the pull—the need—between them, but love? No, Anatoli was mistaken. He confused the heat they shared with love.

Still, it wouldn't do to show the vipers her emotions, no matter what they were—or were not. Annoyed with herself, believing she'd long ago learned to control her features, Katria deliberately blanked her face of the—attraction she felt for Nikolai.

Yes, "attraction" fit perfectly.

"We play the game, Uncle." Carefully choosing her words as they took a few leisurely steps down the spacious hall, she offered a small laugh. "My fate with him is sealed. Nikolai saw to that when he arranged our betrothal." The crowning move in their match: one she had not and did not wish to dispute. "I cannot say it will be a displeasure to marry Count Orlov. I do find him intriguing. But I wouldn't necessarily call it love."

"Whatever it is I see in you, you must control it. You cannot allow others to see this…this emotion. It's dangerous." His hand squeezed hers, one quick movement. "The jealousy of others can be a sharp knife. Keep it hidden. Keep it between the two of you, the soon-to-be Countess Orlov."

Chapter Two

KATRIA SPUN sharply at the new voice, instantly spotting Count Sergey Ivanovitch Radoff and his younger son, Pavel Sergeivitch. They approached with their insidious grins.

True vipers.

Keeping her expression cool, she awaited them. Pavel leered at her, making her skin crawl. Dismissing him with a glare, she turned to his father.

Count Radoff bowed before her, but Katria refused to offer her hand. She wasn't positive she'd receive it back in the same condition— that was, attached. The slight was not unnoticed, but it didn't seem to bother him as he straightened. His light brown hair shimmered in the gilded light, but his dark brown eyes were flat. Although it remained steadily on her, Katria had the impression his gaze took in everything around them. His face was angular, lined around the eyes, with a heavy mustache in the style of the tsar and tsarevich. He held himself tall despite his stout build.

All in all, he served to look both handsome and conniving. Menacing, if she had to choose a word. And yet he'd never done anything overt to cause this suspicion, to have her believe so ill of him.

Pavel Sergeivitch, on the other hand—his look, his glare. He'd always had it, always seemed to be plotting something, Katria thought. It made her uncomfortable. Worse than having her skin crawl. As if she were in some sort of danger.

Several of her friends believed him to be a fine catch despite the fact that he wasn't the eldest son. Katria disagreed, but couldn't persuade them to see things her way.

To Anatoli, Radoff bowed at the waist, right hand touching the floor, then straightened with his right hand over his left, palms upward. "Bless Your Grace."

Anatoli began the sign of the cross and intoned, "May the Lord bless you."

Katria watched him carefully, but he showed no distaste as he placed his right hand in Radoff's hands and Radoff kissed it. She waited while Pavel greeted her uncle as well.

Though this greeting was quick, it needed to be performed every time someone approached Anatoli. She wondered if he tired of it, but she supposed not. He was a bishop in the Church, the living icon of Christ.

"I presume you've heard about Galensky?" Radoff asked Anatoli in his smooth, cultured voice.

"Talk of politics instead of war," Katria interjected, thinking Nikolai certainly passed the information toward Radoff swiftly enough. She nodded toward the doors, where the rest of court congregated. "They speak only of the Oriental War, the latest maneuvers of the English and French in the Ukraine, and the Turkish ships in the Gulf of Finland. Politics is a refreshing change of pace, gentlemen."

"Domestic politics are oftentimes more dangerous than fighting on the front lines," Radoff added.

"I do not disagree," Katria said.

"As can be family politics," Radoff continued. "Which brings me to your betrothal. I've not yet had the chance to congratulate you on the tsar's approval, Countess Markova."

"It's a pity," Pavel spoke up, one of the few times Katria heard him speak. She much preferred his silence.

"Pity?" she forced herself to ask when he said no more.

"Pity that you could not join *our* family." His leer was back, twisting the handsome features he inherited from his father into a grotesque mask of innuendo and intimidation.

Glancing away with a barely concealed sneer of dismissal, Katria smiled at her uncle and Radoff. "I believe Galensky has made his way into the rooms, perhaps we shou—"

"Yes," Radoff interrupted with a parting bow to them. "Yes, I wish to speak with him."

Katria nodded stiffly to Radoff, ignored Pavel completely, and took Anatoli's arm. The two of them walked into the state room, which was hot and noisy, the conversations of three hundred courtiers vying for precedence. Snippets reached her ears, but Katria ignored them all. Despite Anatoli's earlier words about not showing her regard for Nikolai, she couldn't help but search for him now.

She didn't think of herself as the kind of woman to be taken so completely by a man's appearance. She'd met many handsome men before. Court was full of handsome, ambitious men. The way Nikolai held himself, his aloof manner, his Western appearance was so different from many Russians. He wore no mustache, his clothes were cut slightly differently—even his scent was different.

His nearly black eyes seemed to look through her and discover her secrets. Beyond that, his confidence was arrogant, but not, she sensed, unwarranted. Katria knew many arrogant nobles, men and women. In Nikolai, she knew it wasn't misplaced. But she'd never tell him so.

Recognition passed between them at their first meeting. It had been a connection she couldn't explain even now. She'd known his brother, Peter, for years, but hadn't met Nikolai until a few months ago when he returned from Austria.

That meeting changed everything she'd ever thought about herself and her life, awakened a part of her she hadn't known slept. Sharpened her senses. Even made her reckless in her desire for Nikolai.

"I'll see you soon, Uncle," she said, squeezing his arm. Katria moved into the crowd with her well-practiced smile. She nodded in greeting to those she passed and stopped to receive a compliment on her attire or a bit of gossip. Her mind, however, still mused over Nikolai.

It had taken her years and many near misses to assert a semblance of control over her own life. Her father used her ruthlessly. Viktor had promised her at age fifteen to one of the tsar's favorite ministers. The minister had been a diseased old man of sixty-eight, and she'd been saved only when he died mere weeks later. Since then, she'd maneuvered around her father's machinations, skillfully avoiding unwelcome marriages.

Control was what she wanted, and Nikolai was uncontrollable. Her feelings toward him represented a seismic shift in the way she considered her future. Her carefully constructed façade cracked just enough to peer out at him.

Somehow Anatoli knew it, too, when he'd introduced them. One day, she'd ask her uncle about that introduction. And maybe, *maybe* one day she'd ask Nikolai what prompted his proposal.

Now, as she continued across the room, she took this time to find her fiancé. Spotting her dearest friend instead, she stopped.

Making her way through the cluster of people toward Anna Petrovena Tiomkin, Katria caught sight of Nikolai. He slipped through the vipers liked a skilled predator. He was dangerous, of that she had no doubt. His uncle, Count Alexey Fyodorovitch Orlov, headed Russia's secret police, the Third Section. Nikolai's brother, Peter, had no official position within the Third Section, but she'd long ago gathered his diplomatic missions had more to do with them than not.

How deep did Nikolai's connections with the Third Section run?

And Peter, where was he? Nikolai had said he'd return in a few weeks, but his tone implied he knew more about Peter's whereabouts than he let on. Katria longed to see her friend, but nerves bested her over his reappearance in St. Petersburg. Once Peter was in town, there would be no holding off the wedding between her and Nikolai. Her future would begin. The unknown.

Embracing Anna, she glanced about the room.

"Have you heard of Galensky?" Anna asked.

Katria nodded absently, shooting Anna a reproachful glance. Anna laughed, a light breezy sound. "Of course you have," she corrected herself. "When I need to know anything, I should ask you first. Galensky is the latest gossip, but the tsar has yet to make an appearance. There are rumors something is stirring behind closed doors."

"There always are, but it'll be interesting to learn what takes up the tsar's time," Katria agreed.

"Most likely something to do with the war—" Anna cut herself off when Katria took an involuntary step forward. Composing herself, Anatoli's words echoing in her mind, Katria turned to look back at her friend.

"Go." Anna laughed, not the least put off. "We'll dine together tomorrow."

She kissed her friend on the cheek, but Anna held her arm. Looking at Anna, she raised both eyebrows in question.

"How are things between you and Nikolai progressing?"

The smile was there and gone in a flash. Katria had a feeling it expressed more than she wished. Even to Anna, with whom she had grown up, navigated these rooms, and shared her first impressions of Nikolai.

"I'll tell you tomorrow," she promised.

Anna, more serious than was normal, released her arm. "Be careful, Katria."

Nodding at the warning in her friend's voice, she made her way through the crowd to the archway. Nikolai caught her attention and, with a knowing look, vanished from the room.

Discreetly, Katria slipped from the hot and noisy state room. She knew eyes followed her and made certain to pause before a mirror, to look behind her, to check her appearance. Greeting others as they arrived, she headed down the hall.

****

In the empty salon, Nikolai leaned negligently against the gilt gold-and-cream door, arms folded. He didn't care for the décor, but realized, as he awaited Katria, he had missed its distinctly Russian look. He'd been among non-Russians for so long, his former friends accused him of having become Westernized.

If only they knew, he thought. Pushing off the door, he stalked the room, restless. When he returned to St. Petersburg this past summer, he'd done so because his father died. Close to the old man, he knew Andrei Vladivitch silently disapproved of his travels outside the empire.

Upon his return to Russia, Nikolai hadn't expected to meet Katria. European women were beautiful, skilled in the arts of love and court, and yet he'd never met a woman like her. She was beautiful, walked through the tsar's court with her head held high, her pride and reputation intact—to be expected, he supposed, of one in her twentieth year. But she wasn't like others her age. Her soul was older, more astute.

There was something about her, however, that drew his attention as no other woman had. Fleeting though that interest should have been, when Nikolai spoke to her, his fascination—expanded, turned to more.

"Damn it."

Months later, he still couldn't accurately explain what he felt for her.

"Why I have to have you," he muttered into the empty room.

He knew she entered when the din from the courtiers grew louder. Nikolai turned and watched her close the door behind her with a soft click. Defiance and passion lit her eyes, and she tilted her chin as she watched him from across the lavish room. Shoulders back, she stood straight and confident.

The fingers of her left hand twitched in her skirt, the only telltale sign she was anything other than completely composed.

He wanted to shatter that composure, watch her passion consume her. Needed to do so. Wanted to taste that passion, feel her around him as he took her. His own control close to breaking, he smiled wickedly at her. The blue-green of her eyes darkened, deepened. She took a step closer, the break in her pretense widening.

Katria wasn't as immune to him as she pretended.

In two quick steps, he crossed the room and had her in his arms. Before she could react, he kissed her. Beneath him, she opened. Her mouth was hot on his, greedy, taking all he doled out. A small mewl of pleasure vibrated along his lips.

With a growl, he deepened the kiss. Backing her to the wall, uncaring of the voluminous skirts she wore, Nikolai lifted her. Felt her sigh, her fingers in his hair.

Surrender was so close, he could taste it in the sweetness of her kiss.

"Nikolai."

Breathing hard, he pressed his forehead to hers. He wanted to have her now. Kissing down the delicious length of her neck, he knew another crack in the wall surrounding her had chipped open.

"I anticipate having you in my bed every night," he whispered, teeth tugging the lobe of her ear. "Where I can love you whenever I want."

And how he wanted. He wanted her in all ways known to man and woman, wanted to teach her the exquisite sensual arts, to revel in her passion, her desire.

Raising eyes the color of the Black Sea on a beautiful summer's day, she asked, "Is that all you seek from me, Nikolai? My body?"

They were back to the game they played. For every advancement he gained, Katria retreated a step. Setting her to the floor, he still held her, but she pushed back from him with a coy grin. As she walked a few paces away, always sure to keep that distance, Nikolai leaned against the wall and once again folded his arms.

He did love watching her. Always moving, always observing, she seemed to notice everything. Nikolai wondered why she could not see him for what he offered.

Her left hand danced up and down the skirt of her gown, fingers twitching, palm smoothing the heavy material. A knowing smile stretched his lips. *Not as immune as you think, my darling. I'll destroy that pretense yet.*

Stalking up behind her, he moved his fingers up along the string of buttons on the back of her bodice. Pressing his lips to the delicate flesh at the base of her neck, he said, "I want all of you."

She shuddered beneath him.

Turning her, Nikolai met her lips. Beneath the unrestrained passion he had for her, he harbored a need for more. If he could possess her, share in her passion, she'd understand. The wall she'd built around her heart would collapse only for him.

Her taste, her scent—he couldn't absorb enough of it. Their lips crushed against each other's with a power that seduced him, and he knew it did her, as well. She surrendered to him just enough. Deepening the kiss, he challenged the control she held over her emotions. When she resisted, a dissatisfied growl vibrated along her lips. He slipped one hand beneath her bodice, strong fingers stroking the sensitive skin.

With a jagged breath, Katria shuddered again, pulled away. "There will be time enough after we are married."

His fingers tightened on her shoulders, and he saw her wince. Furious with himself for hurting her, with her for denying what lay between them, Nikolai dropped his hands.

"Ah, yes." His tone, laced with sarcasm, stiffened her pride. He watched as she took another step back, tossing her head just enough to prove her point. "I forget how proper and innocent you are."

Eyes narrowed, she took an abrupt step toward him, then stilled. He smirked. *Oh, yes, my darling, I know how to upset that delicate little balance you want in your life.*

"It's no wonder you would forget," she snapped, her voice an odd combination of rigid and scorching. "I'm certain the company you kept before me was anything but *proper* and *innocent*."

Stalking toward her, his anger overriding his control, he grabbed her upper arms, standing a breath away. "I do not recall any company before you."

Damn it, he hadn't meant to say that. But the truth of his words rang in the room. Nikolai watched her take them in, acknowledge them in the shifting of her eyes, the relaxing of her shoulders. She said naught, stood her ground, fought back.

"You needn't worry, you'll have me in your bed soon enough." A challenging bite to her words once again had him appreciating her many facets. "I suppose I should be grateful. You're giving me my own household, relieving me of my father's cold one."

"You will not be cold in my house," Nikolai promised. He hovered over her, unmoving, holding himself as still as a tiger before leaping for its prey.

For months, he'd tried to get through to her, tried to crumble that impenetrable wall, and now, so close to doing so, he felt her slip from his grasp.

"Yes, hmm. Ah…" Stepping back, away from him, she touched her fingers to her forehead.

There. Right there.

Changing the subject, she said, "I spoke to Radoff. He's properly diverted from Khrulev by the Galensky matter."

"Stop." He took her hand. Thumb caressing her through the glove, he waited, watched. "It was there for an instant," he said, "then sealed."

"What?" she asked, confused. Tug though she did, Katria couldn't break his hold, so with a frustrated sigh, she gave up.

"The crack," he said, watching her closely. When she didn't realize it, he noticed she softened, relented. "The crack in your perfectly polished veneer."

Anger rose in her like a flash fire and she snapped, "I shall be more careful and keep my *veneer* intact." Yanking her hand from his, she tilted her chin and glared up at him.

"I don't want what you show everyone else," he said softly, touching her cheek. Again, her eyes changed. "I want what is underneath. I've seen it."

He traced her soft mouth, so at odds with her composure, her words.

"There is nothing underneath."

"*Everything* is underneath." Nikolai tilted his head, forcing her to look at him, really look at him. How long must he wait for that damn shell to crack?

"I can't retain my composure with you, Nikolai." She stepped away, looking around the room rather than at him.

"Why would you want to?" Following her with his gaze, he said, "There are no vipers in here."

With her eyebrow arched, she glanced over her shoulder, "No?"

Smiling, he offered, "None that would bite you." *Trust me, Katria.*

"I cannot be certain of that," she said with confident defiance.

In front of her in a few steps, he trailed his fingers along her neck with a light touch. "Trust your instincts, Katria. Or are they buried under your veneer as well?"

Glancing at the floor, Katria's eyes twinkled when she looked at him through her lashes. "They are suppressed by my desire to see you unclothed."

"A change from a moment ago," he teased, wondering how he had the presence of mind to speak after her words. He hardened at them, aroused by her sensual insinuation.

"A whim," she confessed. Her smile told him otherwise.

"A tactic." He bent to whisper in her ear, teeth nipping her earlobe. "A wicked one, at that." Nikolai chuckled lightly, lips grazing her temple. Pulling back, he winked at her, and opened the door. "I have a surprise for you." He peeked out and frowned when he couldn't see his surprise. "Which should arrive momentarily."

****

Katria saw him shrug as he left the door ajar. In two quick strides, Nikolai re-crossed the room after he caressed her cheek with his fingers. Though his eyes held the passion of a moment ago, his voice had changed, grown lighter.

It galled her to admit he was right: it was a tactic. Needing distance, she wanted to push him back. Could she truly trust him? Reveal herself to him? Part of her said yes, wanted to open to him and take that leap. Part of her, the part that still resided in her father's house, wondered if he just wanted to win.

"I hope I'm interrupting."

Startled, she jerked from Nikolai's arms and moved around him to see the intruder. The tall lieutenant colonel, epaulets and medals gleaming in the soft salon light, laughed. His blue-green eyes warmed as they looked at her, and Katria took a quick step forward, blinking as she saw her brother appear before her.

"Constantine!" she stammered. "What are you...how did you...?"

"I think we rendered her speechless, Nikolai." Constantine laughed. "A feat in and of itself."

Despite huffing, Katria couldn't keep the smile off her face, and even as she swatted her brother's arm, she hugged him close.

"This is a wonderful surprise," she said. Then she laughed, keeping the fear she'd felt for him these years bottled behind her joy at seeing him. "Tell me you're not returning to Sevastopol."

"I've a few weeks here," he said, and she could see the toll of war reflected in his eyes even as his voice remained light.

He kissed the top of her head, a move he'd often done when they were young and he couldn't speak of his feelings. Tears welled in her eyes for what he must have seen and done. He looked older, the lines across his brow and bracketing his mouth deeper than she remembered. She quickly blinked her tears away. Now was not the time.

"Katria." He kissed her cheek. "I know our reunion has been short, but will you please excuse us? I need to speak with Nikolai."

Confused, Katria nodded. This wasn't the greeting she expected. Something was wrong. "Of course," she said and nodded, already backing toward the door.

"Stay." Nikolai's voice cut through the silence that descended on the room.

His gaze locked with hers, and he held out his hand. Without hesitation, Katria crossed to him and took the offered hand, squeezing slightly to show support for whatever Constantine had to say.

She waited as her brother went to the door and double-checked that it remained tightly closed. Once he was assured, he moved back to them.

"What is it?" she asked.

Chapter Three

NIKOLAI LOOKED hard at Constantine Viktorvitch Markova.

The other man looked ashen, the lines around his mouth sharper, deeper. He took a step forward, tentative and so very unlike Constantine. The entire picture looked abnormal, and dread settled in the pit of Nikolai's stomach.

They'd known each other for years, having traveled much of Europe together. When Constantine returned home to join the Imperial Guards, Nikolai continued to travel, uninterested in Russia's military. Politics were his passion, but despite the distance and Constantine's rise through the ranks, they'd maintained a steady friendship.

Beside him, Katria stood silent, waiting for her brother. Her fingers were firm in his, and he took comfort in that, though he didn't know what lay in store.

"What happened?" Nikolai repeated.

"It's Peter."

"What about him?" he demanded, his trepidation from a moment before spreading. "Is he injured?"

"He died last night," Constantine said. "Carriage accident near the Palace."

Peter—dead? Nikolai shook his head, trying to make sense of his friend's words. In the distance, he could hear the noise of the courtiers buzz through the state rooms, and could feel Katria's hand tighten in his. He heard her soft gasp of shock. She and Peter were friendly, he recalled.

Dead. He didn't believe it. "What?" He glanced at Katria, saw the tears in her eyes, making them glitter like jewels. Part of his mind registered her loss of control. "What's going on?" Nikolai shook his head, trying to clear it. This wasn't what he had expected. "How?"

"The carriage overturned—he and the driver were killed." Constantine's voice was low, sympathetic.

"Carriage accident?" Nikolai scoffed. Stepping forward, he dropped Katria's hand and bit out, "My brother is hardly a frail old man to die in an overturned carriage! There must be a mistake. He wasn't due back in St. Petersburg until next month! No, it's not him."

"I was told the light fixture lay beside him, splattered with his blood. His head must have struck the light during the fall. That misfortune took his life."

"Where was he going? What—" Nikolai stopped at his friend's look and narrowed his eyes. "Told by whom?"

"I spoke to Father downstairs in the offices," Constantine said. "As the overseeing minister of the Third Section, he knew before the rumors could start. Someone will officially inform you, but I wanted to tell you myself." He paused, and Nikolai braced himself. "There's more."

More. Suddenly furious, Nikolai paced away. Blinded with rage over what he didn't yet know and the certainty he wouldn't like it, he tried to distance himself from Katria. She was already wary of his passion; if he showed her this, this fury, would she run from him forever?

"Peter is too smart, too quick for such a death." He bit the words off through clenched teeth.

"What was he doing back in St. Petersburg?" Katria looked as if she'd question Constantine further, but stopped and shook her head. Her eyes reflected the same disbelief he felt.

Nikolai tried to think through the grief, shock, the burning anger his brother's death elicited, ran his hands through his hair, but nothing helped. He couldn't comprehend the hows and whys of it all.

Katria's movements were slow as she walked to the settee and collapsed onto it. Standing before her, he looked down into her upturned face, and could see her try to think through everything, to understand it in a way he didn't.

"I have no idea," Nikolai admitted. "Wherever he was, he wasn't due back for weeks. All I know is that he worked to uncover a threat to the war effort."

"Do you think someone followed him back?" she asked. For a moment, he thought she'd retake his hand. Instead, she twisted her fingers into her dress.

"Possibly. I'm not sure. It has to be something along those lines." The fingers of his left hand tapping against his leg, Nikolai tried to puzzle it out. Nothing made sense. "Under no circumstances do I believe the overturned carriage was an accident."

"He was found with treasonous papers." Constantine's words cut through the room.

It took a moment for the meaning to sink in. *Treasonous?* Nikolai slowly turned to look at the other man, unwilling to comprehend what he'd said.

"What the hell are you talking about, Constantine?" he roared. Constantine glanced over his shoulder to make sure no one entered, but Nikolai didn't care. "What papers? What do you mean? Treason? Impossible!"

"Peter Orlov is *not* a traitor!" Katria jumped off the settee, pointing a finger at Constantine. "I'd sooner believe the tsar himself passed secrets." She turned to Nikolai, voice firm with conviction. "I know your brother. You may have spent your time abroad, but he was here in St. Petersburg, at court. Anatoli trusted him and I saw his loyalty with my own eyes. It's an insidious, vicious lie spread by one of those damn vipers. I wouldn't put it past any of them." Her eyes danced with fury and she stabbed a finger toward the doors blocking out those in the state rooms. "There are very few here I believe would put Russia above anything else, especially their own ambitions. He was one. Peter put Russia before anything."

Pacing away again, she shook her head, muttering more of the same under her breath. Turning back around, she said, "There have been plots against your family for more than a hundred years!"

"Peter isn't a traitor. He has sacrificed more for the tsar than I can share." Nikolai looked over at Katria, and saw how flushed she was, how angry. Her anger rivaled his own. *I knew she was my match.*

"What did these papers say?" he snapped. "What else did Viktor say?"

"The Third Section was called in after the accident," Constantine admitted. His friend hadn't moved from where he stood, guarding the door as he and Katria talked. Now he walked closer, keeping his voice quiet.

"Isn't that standard when a member of the nobility dies?" Katria sounded relieved. "Nikolai, your uncle is head of the Third Section. I'm certain they'll investigate Peter's death and look into all avenues of inquiry."

"I suppose. But Alexey is unreachable, also out of the country." Nikolai needed to control himself. He refused to let his emotions boil over into uncontrollable rage. Peter had been his closest friend; only Constantine came close to sharing that level of trust.

"Perhaps..." She hesitated, and he wondered what she wanted to say. He watched as she took a deep breath and met his gaze. "Perhaps we can ask Father to investigate."

Surprised by this offer, as Katria wasn't usually one to involve her father, Nikolai nodded.

"Who else knows of this?" she asked her brother. "What did Father tell you?"

"The papers found with Peter indicated he may have been involved in sensitive financial matters within the Turkish borders. As far as I know," Constantine admitted, "that information is staying between Father, me, Lazarenko, Terenov, and now you two."

Frowning, Katria moved closer to Nikolai. "Financial matters? They could have been in place before the war. What exactly do they indicate?"

"I haven't seen the papers myself," Constantine said, and Nikolai dreaded what came next. "However, they may associate Peter with... questionable dealings."

"Questionable?" Katria snorted in relief. "Constantine, there are few things in Russia that *aren't* questionable. Politics are our life. We're raised on intrigue. Every courtier in this Palace has something *questionable* about him."

"On the surface, Father said, the papers aren't proof of treason, but they do raise questions." Constantine approached Nikolai. "Peter's dead. I've convinced Father that it makes no further difference. I agree with you that Peter was no traitor. But the best course of action now is to conceal it and all else you may find associated with these matters."

Numb, Nikolai nodded. In his darkest nightmares, he hadn't thought something this destructive could happen. The Orlovs had a pristine reputation with the tsar. Katria's voice brought him back to the matter at hand.

"Constantine," he heard her say. "Can you give us a moment?"

The door closed and they were once again alone. Focusing, Nikolai saw her standing before him. Her warm hand cupped his cheek. "I'm sorry," she whispered.

He took her hand, holding it for a heartbeat. In a move too swift to give her time to protest, he pulled her into his arms. Laying his cheek against the top of her head, he tried to think. His chest tightened with grief, but he ruthlessly tamped it down. Anger overrode grief, and he embraced it.

"Treason—it's a lie against Peter."

She met his gaze. "I know."

Katria's utter acceptance snapped something in Nikolai. Crushing her to him, he sought her lips. She eagerly kissed him back, meeting his grief-fueled passion. With a growl, he picked her up, walking until her back hit the wall.

Looking down at her bright eyes, he retook her lips, needing to feel something—her—needing to claim her. Part of his life was ripped away with Peter's death. He wanted to fill the void with her. He didn't want to let her go, wanted to take her home. It was too soon.

But restraining himself, Nikolai managed, "I'm sorry."

"It's all right," she said. Then, before he could walk away, she wrapped her arms around him and held him close.

****

Katria closed the door to her room, grateful no one questioned her. Leaning against it, she took a moment, the wood sturdy behind her. The silk wallpaper draping the walls and lush landscape paintings from Russia's romantic history, once soothing, did little to ease the tension coiling within her.

Crossing to the far side of the room, she flung open the curtains. Struggling with the window, she inched it up enough to breathe in the cold air. With the wind seeping through, chilling her fingers, she knelt, resting her cheek against the sill.

Dread settled around her. Despite what she showed Nikolai, what she said to him, she was anxious. She truly believed in Peter's innocence. But fear of what the rumors would do—what the vipers would do—to Nikolai and his family sent ice through her veins. If the Orlovs were lucky, if there was a grain of truth in those papers, they'd devour Nikolai. If they weren't lucky, the vipers would utterly destroy them. Take Nikolai away from her.

She had to help him.

Her father knew already, but what would he do? What would he really do with the information? Could Constantine keep it all a secret?

Yes, she knew her brother well enough to know he could. Her father would not, could not, interfere. Nikolai would be safe from whatever Peter's papers contained as long as no one else was involved.

Going from flirting and toying with Nikolai to something completely different, she could pinpoint the moment things changed between them. But was the change anything more than sympathy?

"I don't want to lose him," she whispered into the empty room.

Regardless of Nikolai's efforts to "crack her veneer," now everything was different. One thing she was certain of: whatever she could do to help him, be it to avenge Peter's death or to skirt the lies already spreading about him, she would.

A quick rap at her door brought her to the present. Struggling off the floor, she crossed the room. Anna stood in the hallway, looking flushed, anxious.

"Anna?" she asked, wondering if she was meant to dine with Anna this eve or not. Their conversation seemed a lifetime ago.

Her friend rushed by her, glancing over her shoulder as she closed the door. "I must talk with you."

"What's happened?" She feared she knew the answer, but turned the key in the lock nonetheless.

"It's all over court," Anna breathed in a rush, only now untying her cloak. "Scandal associated with Nikolai's brother—with his death. No one knows why he was in St. Petersburg when he wasn't expected this winter. Some have even hinted it may not have been an accident."

"Has there been any more talk? Have you heard anything else?" she demanded, squeezing Anna's arm harder than she intended. When her friend winced, Katria let go and stepped back.

"No, that's all I heard. Why, Katria?" she asked. "Have you heard something else?"

"No," she said, shaking her head and cursing herself for the slip even though she trusted Anna implicitly. "No, nothing else." She stumbled over the words. "I don't want Nikolai bothered by these horrid rumors."

"You suddenly seem very protective of him," Anna said. Was that a hint of suspicion in her voice? Or Katria's imagination? "What a change in the few hours since I've seen you."

Slowly, Katria admitted, "I was with Nikolai when he learned about Peter. He's devastated by his brother's death." Desperately wanting to tell Anna what happened between them, all she allowed was, "And so I am protective of him, Anna. I am...sympathetic."

Anna studied her for a moment. "I think it's more than that," she said eventually. "I think you feel more than sympathy. Your tone has changed."

Katria watched her eyes narrow, saw her take a step forward.

Had things changed? Anna had asked what she'd wondered herself. "I'm not insensitive to his situation. Since we are to marry..." she said, and knew she prattled on when she should keep her mouth shut. Katria was afraid she'd reveal too much. "We'll need to move past what we currently have."

"You're not concerned?" Anna asked. She moved so she could see Katria's face, and Katria knew she was caught. Her friend knew her all too well. "Not concerned about his 'darkness,' as you called it?"

"No." The word was simple, elegant in its simplicity. Having surprised herself with that answer, she repeated, "No. I'm not."

When she said no more, Anna nodded. Her mind whirling with thoughts of Nikolai and Peter, Katria once more gripped her friend's arm. "Anna, please do something for me."

"Anything," her friend immediately agreed.

Katria breathed a sigh at Anna's ready acceptance. "Return to court. Please listen to whomever wishes to talk about Peter Orlov. I need to know everything they do about his death."

Though she did dislike speaking with many of the more vicious at court, Anna nodded.

"Thank you," Katria said, kissing her cheek as she walked her friend to the door. She had to plan. A sick feeling in her stomach told her Peter's death was only the beginning.

Chapter Four

February 7, 1855
Georgian Calendar

NIKOLAI SAT behind his desk in the too-quiet house. In the background, servants wandered, cleaning, dusting, keeping well out of his way. Though Peter hadn't been here in months, it was only now that he was forever gone that their family home seemed too large, too silent.

Closing the account books and locking them in the desk drawer, Nikolai hoped the bribe he'd paid was enough. Hell, he'd have paid three times as much to keep this information about his beloved brother secret. He hadn't heard back from Uncle Alexey despite the message he'd sent and the courier he'd bribed to carry it no matter where the man currently was. What infuriated him was the mere fact of these rumors. It went against everything he knew about Peter.

Was it even worth pursuing? In the aftermath of Peter's death and funeral, when he had time to think, Nikolai wondered. If his investigation into Peter's activities sparked something against him, it would fall on the entire family—now on him, the sole survivor of this branch of the Orlov line.

He'd lose his honor, his name, his position. He'd lose Katria.

That was something he didn't want to contemplate.

Where was she? He'd become used to seeing her here every day since Peter's death. Already mid-afternoon, she'd yet to visit him. She'd changed in the few days between their last encounter in the Palace and now. More at ease with him, more open. Less controlled.

Her own sorrow at Peter's death made her vulnerable; he wasn't certain she realized that about herself, but he wasn't going to test her. Yet.

Scrubbing a hand over his face, Nikolai stood. He looked forward to their marriage when she'd be here all the time. When, hopefully, no barriers would exist between them.

As if his thoughts conjured her, Katria slipped into the study and quietly closed the door.

"Are you all right?" he asked, just resisting the urge to move to her.

"There was a message from Father but I didn't manage to speak with him. I wanted to see you," she admitted with a smile.

"You risked Viktor's wrath for me?" He grinned with the half smile he knew threw her off kilter. He wanted her unbalanced, when she was more apt to open up.

"You seem relaxed," she teased. Her smile was brilliant, and it warmed him.

Taking her hand, he tugged her into his arms. She laughed, and he lightly kissed her in greeting; a playful maneuver he wanted to deepen. But when she looked up at him, eyes shining with amusement, Nikolai found he couldn't spoil the moment. Instead, he grinned again, and watched her eyes drop to his mouth, her tongue peeking out to moisten her full lips.

Intense satisfaction surged through him. He wouldn't push. These last several days they had shared an easy interaction, and he didn't want to return to the way it was before. The feeling between them now was what he craved.

"I am. I believe I've taken care of the papers found with Peter." Katria nodded, and he knew she already understood what he'd done. "I'm looking forward to having you in this house."

She released a heavy breath, fingers dancing over his cheek. Swallowing, she admitted, "I am, too."

Nikolai blinked at her declaration. Before she had a chance to break away, to close herself off, he kissed her. She accepted his kiss, even kissed him back, but despite her words, there was still a hesitance between them. He wasn't surprised when she pulled away.

"Peter's death is no longer the main topic at court," she said, wandering the room. She trailed her fingers along his desk, the books lining the walls.

So they were back to this, were they? Nikolai nodded, arms folded as he watched her. *So close.*

"Thank you for relaying the information," he said formally.

"Are you angry with me, Nikolai?" she asked, surprised.

"Angry?" he repeated. Was he? "I've more to consider than your games, Katria." Yes, he was angry. He could taste the difference in her kiss, but she refused to yield control of her emotions.

Stalking to his desk, he nodded toward the door. "I have other business to attend to. In fact, I have an appointment this afternoon with your uncle."

"Anatoli?" She nodded in understanding. "Nikolai, don't be cross with me. I do care and only want what's in your best interest. Our reputations will be entwined soon enough."

Her words angered him, as talk of Peter's so-called treasonous activities had not. He didn't believe Peter was a traitor. But Katria…he thought he knew *her*, not this talk of reputations. What lay beneath, who she truly was. He wanted that woman.

Perhaps she was merely a fantasy, one he'd made up to prove to himself—and her—she wasn't as cold and callous as she appeared.

"I had hoped," he spat, "you'd consider more than our reputations."

She moved beside him, took his hand. "Oh, I do, Nikolai." The words were reluctant, but he sensed the honesty in them. Pausing, he looked down at her. "I consider the enjoyment we'll extract from our marriage to be a significant benefit."

His fingers tightened around hers, and he released a heavy sigh. *She wanted to play the game? Fine.*

Backing her against the desk, he closed the distance between them. He traced the square neckline of her gown, felt her shudder at the touch. Katria arched against him, and he knew it was involuntary, knew her control threatened to shatter.

"You're correct, Katria. I look forward to tasting you." His lips stopped a hair's breadth from hers. Her eyes darkened, her breath uneven. His fingers dipped beneath her bodice, teased her breasts. "Look forward to taking you."

In a move that surprised him, she leaned forward and nipped his lower lip. Her voice was sultry and heat speared through him. "*There is my Nikolai.*"

Her nails scratched down his neck, sending arousal shooting through him. Her fingers moved over his chest to the waistband of his pants.

"You do not want to continue this," he said. "If you push me, I'll lose all restraint."

Just as she looked on the verge of accepting, Katria laughed and pushed him away. "Anatoli is in the parlor," she said. "And I need to return home."

Her hand was on the door when he whirled her around. "Be careful of the games you play, my love. They can be dangerous."

Smile soft, eyes knowing, she leaned up and kissed him. "I know."

She slipped out of the study and he heard her laughing with Anatoli. As the bishop entered the room, Nikolai had the distinct impression Katria felt, *saw*, even more than he realized.

****

Sergey Radoff entered the Markova house. As one of the oldest townhouses in St. Petersburg, and designed by Peter the Great's chief architect Jean-Baptiste Alexandre Le Blond, he'd long admired its grandeur. Standing in the columned foyer, he handed his overcoat to the servant and followed the butler to where Viktor Markova waited.

Markova stood by the windows, clearly awaiting his arrival. "Count Markova." Sergey bowed in greeting.

"Radoff." Markova bowed. "Shall we skip the preliminaries?"

"Of course," he said. This was better. Necessary though it was, he detested wading through niceties. He admired a man who could come straight to the point and know what that point was. "I'm here to talk about your daughter's future."

"Oh?" he said, no emotion showing on his face. "What interest could that be of yours?"

"We're two great families here. *Russian* families." Sergey gestured outside the room, including the city, implying the entire country. "Joining our families, our resources, will be to both our benefits."

"Hmm, I see. As I'm sure you're aware, Radoff, Katria is already betrothed."

"I'm quite aware of her current status." Sergey shrugged. "As I'm also *aware* of the possible problems hanging over the Orlov family."

"You aren't a member of the Third Section," Markova said in an even voice as he walked to the desk. But Sergey knew he had the other man's complete attention. "How did you come by this information?"

"My dear Markova." Sergey shook his head. "The secret police are, at times, not so secretive. I've come into this information as any diligent courtier would."

Markova's hands slammed on his desk. Perfect, a sign of weakness. "How many others know of this. . .this unsubstantiated information?"

"Very few," Sergey assured him with a knowing smile. "So far. But I can't imagine the information will stay unknown much longer."

The other man nodded, hands clasped behind his back as he wandered to the liquor tray. "Should Katria's engagement be broken," he said slowly, "she won't be ready for any new arrangements so quickly. She'll need time to adjust."

"Women adjust more swiftly than you give them credit for," Sergey said, undeterred. He took a step closer, smiling sympathetically. "The Orlov family might be tainted by this scandal. Would you not rather her be associated with someone with a sterling reputation? Your name, after all, is all you have in court."

He paused, letting his implication sink in, though he was positive a man as judicious as Viktor Markova didn't need but an instant to change his course. If he wished to play their conversation this way, Sergey would play along.

"I'm willing to join forces with the Markova name," Sergey continued. "A wedding announcement between Katria and Mikhail will effectively dissociate you from the Orlovs."

Markova raised an eyebrow. Not as intimidating as his brother, Anatoli, Viktor nonetheless possessed a blank stare that rivaled Sergey's own. Impressive. Shaking his head, the other man strode a step forward.

"I don't want something like this perceived badly by the tsar." His words were measured, and Sergey couldn't decide if they were meant to stall him or not. "He did, in fact, give his approval to Katria's union with Orlov."

"We can wait a *short* time," Sergey conceded, something he'd already planned on doing. "Therefore not affronting the tsar with this new betrothal. Give the girl time to come to terms with her broken engagement, get used to marrying Mikhail."

"I'm not saying she won't," Viktor said. "Yet I have not agreed. I'll consider your proposition, Radoff. But you'll have no answer from me until after Lent."

"Take some time," he smiled. It was no matter. He knew he had the other man. Just to warn him he added, "My offer will not remain open forever. Mikhail will want a bride. And I," he said, smiling, "I want grandchildren."

****

Katria walked into the study, an unexpected ball of ice settling in her stomach. She never dreaded meeting her father, but seeing Sergey Radoff leave the house and her father's almost instant summons made her uneasy.

"Father?" She closed the door behind her, straightened her shoulders, and prepared for this interview. "What was *that* man doing here?"

"We discussed you, Katria."

She knew where this was going. She had guessed the moment Radoff entered the house, and did not want to hear it. For one brief moment, she thought perhaps her father would toss him out on his ear. But no, not Viktor Mikhailivitch Markova. He never went so far to protect her.

Of all the times she wished Anatoli was her father, there was no time she wished it more than now.

"I don't want to hear this. I'm certain," she snapped in her haughtiest voice, "there's nothing you could have discussed with Radoff that interests me. I need to tend to Mother."

It was an old excuse, but one she used often. Her mother was not herself, hadn't been for as long as Katria could remember. Tending to her gave Katria space to breathe, time to think.

"Sit." The command stopped her where she stood near the door. This was worse than she expected.

In three long strides, he'd crossed the room and gripped her arm, shoving her toward a chair opposite his desk. Stumbling against the arm, she straightened but did not sit. Defiant, she raised her gaze to meet her father's.

"I'm considering a betrothal between you and Mikhail Radoff," he said. Through narrowed eyes, Katria could see the anger threaten to show itself. Part of her wished to see his temper explode, but this was not the time. No, this was far too important for such petty thoughts.

Katria knew this was coming; she knew him. She had always known what kind of man he was.

"My engagement to Nikolai," she paused, "has been approved by Tsar Nicholas himself. We have every permission and every right to marry."

She swallowed at the fear of losing Nikolai.

"You still require your *father's* permission," he said.

"Do I?" she bit out. Stomach clenching, she refused to consider his threat. "How unfortunate. What has Radoff said to you to bring about this change of heart?"

"It is not your position to question me, child. You do as I say. Do what is best for this family and our name."

She shook her head, steeling herself against his rejection, his unswerving loyalty to the Markova name, status, and position. "The Orlov name still has its influence. Nothing has come out to defile them. Why would you take such a precipitous move now, to insult them in front of the tsar?"

Viktor was before her again, his cold fingers on her chin so she couldn't avoid him. "I don't want to hear another word about Orlov. You do what is best for our family and our name. I will not justify my reasoning to you."

Jerking her chin from his grip, Katria gathered her skirts and walked backward around the chair, never letting him out of her sight.

"Leave this decision in my hands," he said.

Still watching him as she backed out of the door, Katria considered for a heartbeat grabbing the poker and smashing it over her father's head. No. Whirling, she ran to the stairs and paused on the third step. Racing back down the steps, she rang for a servant and quickly bundled herself into her cloak as the carriage was brought back around.

"Nikolai Orlov's," she commanded, slamming the door closed before the driver could react.

Shaking from anger, her hands ice, she tried to compose herself. This was not her, displaying emotion like this. Yet she could not control the trembling of her limbs and was grateful she sat in the warmth of the carriage.

"Damn it," she muttered, breathing deeply to manage her emotions. "Damn it!"

Never had her father's drive and ambition cut through her so deeply. Her stomach twisted at the thought of the Radoffs. Like a rat from a sinking ship, Viktor had abandoned Nikolai. He obviously had no wish to help the Orlovs.

But with the Radoffs? Especially knowing how she felt about them, it was sickening.

Pulling the curtain back just enough to look out the window, Katria watched the city pass by. Several people braved the icy sidewalks to shop along Nevsky Prospekt. Even with the shortages caused by the Turkish ships blockading the city, the shop owners always had wares to sell. They passed Trinity Square, rounding Kamennoostrovsky Prospekt.

Despite second guessing herself, Katria resisted telling the driver to turn around, or seeking out Anatoli instead. This was something even her beloved uncle could not help her with. Trusting her instincts, she let the driver continue to Nikolai's residence.

Not soon enough, the carriage slowed before his townhouse. He stood on the steps, dressed for the outdoors. She wondered if this was indeed a bad idea.

Letting the curtain fall back over the window, Katria took a moment to compose herself. Before she could, however, the door wrenched open.

"Katria?"

"I had to talk to you," she admitted, taking his hand to descend the steps.

He caught her about the waist, holding her close. Though confident her legs could carry her, Katria said nothing and allowed Nikolai to help her across the walkway. Cursing her pounding heart and stinging emotions, Katria nonetheless leaned on him.

Too soon, they were inside. Hands on her shoulders, he turned her to face him. "Katria?" One hand cupped her face and she swore real concern colored his voice. "What is it?"

"Radoff came to see Father today," she admitted in a rush. "Seeking my hand for his son, Mikhail."

"Son of a bitch," Nikolai spat, hands tightening on her shoulders. "He knows of the papers Peter carried." She nodded, but he didn't see it. "We'll have to find out who else knows."

"Radoff bribes anyone and everyone. I'm sure someone in the Third Section told him." She slapped her fists against her skirt. Given the voluminous width of it, however, Katria didn't feel any pain or satisfaction for the action.

"I paid off the two Constantine named, Lazarenko and Terenov. The papers are safely locked away until Uncle Alexey returns, and Anatoli confirmed it—Alexey is unreachable. Damn it!" Nikolai cursed, stalking to the fireplace. "How the hell could he know anything?"

"Either Radoff has seen them or he's managed to acquire a page or pages. It wouldn't surprise me if that vulture descended on the carriage while Peter's body was still inside."

"If that's true, I'll snap his neck. However, anything coming out of Radoff's hand will be suspicious," he pointed out, a contemplative look on his handsome face.

"Father didn't confirm," she began, trying to remember her father's words. Panic colored the memory. "He didn't confirm he broke our engagement, but he implied he would. I think it's a matter of time—and not a lot of time—before he actually does."

Katria searched his face for a reaction to her declaration. She saw anger, but wasn't sure if it was about Peter or her father's threat.

"We'll deal with our broken engagement *if* it comes to pass," he said. "I may still be able to handle the situation without scandal."

Chapter Five

February 10, 1855
Georgian Calendar

"WHO DID you tell?" His tone even, Nikolai slid the knife into the man's thigh.

To anyone overhearing their conversation, they'd never suspect he'd just sank a blade into Lazarenko's leg.

Of course, they were in the man's own study, with only the servants to overhear. Nikolai had no use for niceties. He needed answers and needed them now. He would not give up Katria. Whatever Peter was or was not involved in, the rumors surrounding his death needed to be put to rest.

"No one!" Lazarenko cried. "I swear I told no one!"

"I paid you handsomely to maintain silence. How the hell did this information fall into Radoff's hands?"

"On the life of the tsar," Lazarenko swore, sweat beading his forehead, blood pouring from his leg. "I do not know!"

Nikolai yanked the knife from his thigh, contemplating his words. The second-in-command of the Third Section, while a skilled spy, did not handle pain well.

"The papers were sequestered in my office since just after his death," Lazarenko continued. "Only Terenov, myself, and Count Markova know of their existence."

"Then perhaps," Nikolai said, "I need to have a conversation with Terenov."

Wiping the bloody knife on Lazarenko's coat, he slashed through the man's bonds. "See that no one accesses the papers. Alexey will manage the situation when he returns."

Nikolai left the gasping man in his own desk chair. He paused as another thought occurred to him and rounded the chair from which Lazarenko hadn't moved. "What was Peter working on?"

"I don't know," the man stammered. Nikolai toyed with the knife, watching as the other man's eyes followed its movements. "He wasn't working for us."

That gave Nikolai pause. Then for whom *had* he worked?

Opening the door to find Lazarenko's servants hovering in the hallway, he jerked his head back into the study. "Your master needs a bandage. See to it."

As they scurried to do his bidding, Nikolai shrugged on his coat and left.

Rage drove him to ride the distance across the city. Now, as he mounted his horse, a prized Orlov trotter from Uncle Alexey's farm, and rode back to his townhouse, he wondered if Markova and Radoff conspired against him. Conspired to wrench Katria from him.

They'd both pay. Fury ripped through him. They would not use the death of a brother he loved dearly to take away the one woman he wanted beyond all reason. Even with the games they played, or maybe because of them, he needed her.

He could still taste her, the tang of her skin, the lushness of her lips. Even the cold wind whipping through the streets could not dim his want of her. Aroused at the thought, the memory of Katria in his arms, he spurred his horse faster.

Katria.

His biggest fear was that she would shut down, withdraw from him, when he was so close to gaining all he desired from her, and she to giving in to him.

He could not lose her; he needed her more than he imagined he ever would another.

There had to be more just under the surface he wasn't seeing. Did this have to do with what Peter worked on in Europe? Was it connected on a personal level? A scheme against his family? Against Uncle Alexey or his son? Something to keep him and Katria apart?

If the latter were the case, then everything pointed back to Radoff. He'd be the only one to gain. It was common knowledge Radoff wanted Markova's support to gain a seat on the Council of Ministers—with Galensky stepping down, this was his perfect opportunity. But would Radoff really move against Peter, indeed the entire Orlov family? Or was it just a lucky coincidence for that son of a bitch?

Whatever the truth, he intended to find out.

****

Pavel Radoff lounged before the fireplace in his father's study, tumbler of vodka in his hand, one leg over the arm of the leather chair. Sergey paced the room, his own glass of vodka forgotten on the mantel. Pavel eyed it, but decided it was too far away. Leaning his head against the chair, he waited for his father's continued tirades against the Orlovs.

"Why are you giving her to Mikhail?" he asked as his father picked up his glass and downed its contents in one swallow. Damn. Missed his chance.

"I want her in one piece for a while," Sergey snapped, "and I know, Pavel, in what direction your proclivities lie."

Snorting, not in the least offended at the truth, Pavel said, "Mikhail won't know what to do with her." He heaved himself off the chair and poured more vodka. "Still, it was clever taking advantage of the situation against Orlov."

"The lands Viktor will bestow with her marriage are more than enough compensation for having that woman in this house."

"Where did you discover this information?" Mikhail asked from before the windows.

He held the curtain back with one hand, watching the street as if it offered anything interesting. Pavel also noticed with disgust that his dear brother had no vodka, limiting himself to one glass a day. Pathetic, weak Mikhail, who couldn't hold his liquor.

"Our friends in the Third Section," Sergey answered absently, once more stalking the room.

"We know Peter was a traitor. They had written proof. You've always eyed her, Mikhail, I've seen it," Pavel taunted. "She's a beautiful woman." And one he wouldn't mind bedding himself. He imagined her all too easily tied to his bed. Mikhail would share her. Pavel would see to it that he hadn't a choice in the matter once he married the Markova bitch.

"We've never had that kind of friendship, Pavel," Mikhail snapped.

"Well, now," their father cut in, "you will."

"We needn't play these games." Mikhail retorted. "Nikolai probably had no knowledge, and I doubt Peter committed treason. For that matter, anyone in the Orlov family, much less *Alexey* Orlov, would do so. Whatever proof those idiots you bribed at the Third Section say they have, I'm sure it's locked away, far from our reach."

Swallowing another sip of alcohol, Pavel laughed at his brother when Sergey slapped him across the face. One, two, three vicious smacks, jerking his head back to bang against the window. Blood welled on Mikhail's lip, but the older brother didn't flinch or release his grip on the opened curtain, too used to the beatings their father inflicted upon him. Sergey tried that once with Pavel, but when he'd only laughed and asked for more, the old man stopped.

"Your justifications are unimportant, Mikhail," Sergey snapped. "It's never about truth, but always about what you can acquire."

"Father—"

"Quiet!" Sergey shouted. "You will do as I command."

"What's our next move?" Pavel asked, more out of boredom than an interest in his father's plans.

"The tsar's approval is an issue," Sergey mulled aloud. "Or maybe not. Nicholas is preoccupied with matters of war. These last defeats have weighed heavily on him. It's unlikely he'll object to a matter as trivial as this."

****

Katria took extra care with her appearance this morning. Seeing Nikolai was a distinct possibility, and she looked forward to it. Smoothing down the deep burgundy of her velvet gown, she adjusted the sleeves under her jacket, though they lay perfectly against her arms.

With a deep breath, she left her room, the first time she'd done so in two days, since her father told her of his conversation with Sergey Radoff. Sequestering herself at home, with only her manipulative father and mad mother for company, she'd gone slightly insane herself. But as Nikolai worked to clear Peter's name and discover how Radoff knew of the so-called treasonous papers, Katria hadn't wanted to risk seeing any of that family.

Constantine spent most of his time at the Winter Palace doing whatever it was he did. In truth, Katria wasn't certain why her brother was in St. Petersburg. Nikolai had said he had a surprise for her that long ago morning at court. Had he arranged Constantine's stay here? Or was it a happy coincidence gone awry? Either way, she hadn't seen her brother since Peter's funeral.

Now, as she stepped from her room and carefully walked down the steps, she gathered everything Anatoli ever taught her. It felt, she realized as she tied her cloak and a servant held open the door, a bit like the armor Peter the Great wore. Except she protected herself with wits and cleverness rather than steel.

The ride to the Palace was interminable, yet the instant she stepped into the state rooms, she knew it hadn't been long enough. With one glance, she could find no ally in the immediate vicinity. Head held high, façade firmly in place, she stepped into the viper's nest.

Instantly, she was besieged.

"Countess Markova," Princess Ulensky said in a staged whisper. "I'm so very sorry. And you two on the very brink! You must be devastated."

"What do you mean?" Katria asked, dreading the answer she already knew. By now, a crowd had gathered around them, whispers jumping from one to the next to the next. The din rose, and Katria's heart pounded.

"My dear." The princess took her hand in a gesture of sympathy the old bat had never displayed to anyone. "You can't possibly go through with the wedding now!"

Damn her father! What had he said? What had he implied? Worse, what rumors did Radoff spread?

"I heard the proof had been lost." Princess Ulensky looked around as if they could have a private conversation in the middle of the Palace with half the room looking on. "I have my suspicions as to *how* it was lost."

She implied Alexey Orlov had a hand in the disappearance of this mysterious proof. Katria kept her mouth shut. Defending Nikolai would do no good, and she'd sound as desperate to clear his name as she felt.

"Without it, the tsar can't move against either him or the family," the woman continued. "I supposed it would be irrelevant, since Peter is dead."

Katria raised her chin and swept her cold gaze around the crowd murmuring and agreeing with the princess. Across the room, Tsar Nicholas sat silently watching the exchange.

"If I were you," the princess added, "I'd dissociate myself from him as quickly as possible. All traitors, the lot of them, I say!"

"I'm sure you do, Princess." Katria nodded. "I've seen your loyalty flap as a flag does in the wind."

With that, Katria turned and descended the steps, back straight, walking slowly and sedately, never rushing, never showing how much the entire conversation upset her. She was stronger than that.

"Katria," Anna said, slipping her arm through Katria's. "I've looked everywhere for you! I should have known you'd be at the center of that horrible crowd."

"I'm leaving now, Anna," she said, her voice strained.

"You're not upset over what Ulensky said to you?" Anna demanded, but continued to walk down the Jordan staircase with her.

"Of course not," she snapped. "Not what the old woman said, but what they all implied. They've already spurned Nikolai, dismissed him from the graces of court. Damned him with proof none of them has and no one's seen!"

It was difficult to breathe, as if the air was sucked from the room. "I need to leave," Katria whispered.

"I know." Anna nodded. "I called for my carriage. It should be here momentarily. When I couldn't find you here, I was going to look for you at your house."

The servant already held Anna's cloak and with the incentive of several rubles rushed to get Katria's as well. Controlling her breathing, she waited, Anna silent beside her. The instant the servant returned with her cloak, they left.

The driver slammed the door shut and Katria lost control. The sob tore through her, and no matter how she tried, she couldn't control her angry tears.

"They've already passed judgment on him and have nothing! They know nothing!" she cried.

"It will pass, Katria," Anna assured her, desperately patting her hand. "It will pass. Nikolai will restore his good name."

Wiping the tears from her cheeks, she turned to her friend. "It may be too late."

"Too late?" Anna demanded. "I don't understand."

"Father's threatened to marry me to Mikhail Radoff. This is his opening." She took Anna's now limp hand and pressed it tightly between her two.

Anna looked ill, and Katria felt rage well anew at her father and Sergey Radoff.

"I'm sorry, Anna. I'm sorry. You know I don't want to. But I fear Father and Radoff are conspiring to make it happen, and nothing I or Mikhail say will prevent it. I'm sorry," she repeated. "I want Nikolai."

The instant the words left her lips, Katria knew them to be true. She *only* wanted Nikolai, despite her fears. Fears she now realized were unjustified. He'd never hurt her; no, what she feared was that she'd lose her control, that which she held most precious, in the depth of wanting him.

The carriage jolted to a halt, and Katria glanced out the window. Nikolai's house. Anna's doing. Hugging her friend, she asked, "Anna? I know you and Mikhail tried to arrange something between you. If it's in my power to prevent this marriage, I will. You know that."

"I know," Anna whispered, snapping out of her shock. "Katria, be careful. Court is capricious, but the tsar isn't as forgiving."

Kissing her friend's cheek, Katria said, "I must find a way to help Nikolai. I can't lose him. I need another favor."

The color back in her cheeks, Anna said in a firmer voice, "Anything."

"Go back to court and find out what else they know. Or think they do."

"Done. I'll visit you tonight, your father. . . he doesn't know about Mikhail and me, and still thinks my family has much to offer in exchange for our friendship. He won't bar me from your house."

"No." Katria choked out a laugh. Despite the nonchalant air she projected to the rest of the world, Anna was the strongest person she knew.

With one last kiss on her friend's cheek in thanks, Katria climbed out of the carriage.

Chapter Six

NIKOLAI BROKE off his conversation with Constantine the instant the door slammed open. He'd heard a carriage, but hadn't bothered to look out the window. Light footsteps raced across the foyer, and he knew Katria had entered. Throwing open the study doors to greet her, he was met with the sight of her tear-stained face.

Fury at whoever or whatever caused her to cry shot through him like a bullet. Katria halted steps from him, wisps of hair falling from one of the elaborate buns she wore, eyes luminous with tears in the gaslight, breasts heaving as she struggled to catch her breath.

"They know." He said the words simply, heart twisting at the sight of her tears.

Tears for him. Drawing her into his arms, Nikolai tucked her head under his chin and held her. She trembled, but did not cry.

"I came straight from the Palace," she admitted in a quiet voice.

"Constantine told me before dawn," he acknowledged, jerking his head to where her brother stood. Leaning back, he took her shoulders, rubbing his thumbs over the pulse point at the base of her neck. Even with all that was going on, he wanted her.

"There's no proof," Constantine said. "Between the two of us, we'd already managed to conceal the papers they'd found."

"Lazarenko was extremely helpful," Nikolai added with a grin.

Drawing her into the study and to the fireplace, he untied her cloak and took her bare hands. In her rush, it seemed she'd neglected to put on her gloves. Rubbing her fingers between his, Nikolai debated how much to tell her. Another look at her determined face, incensed with these rumors, decided for him.

What she exposed clearly convinced him she was invested in them, in their relationship. The rumors cut her just as deeply as they cut him. The sincerity she displayed touched him.

"We're trying to track the origin of the rumor," he said. "I'm confident we can squash it, but we've yet to discover the trail."

"They already condemn you, Nikolai." She rubbed the tears on her face, composure fully returned. "They'll devour you to serve their own ambitions."

"Not the least of them will be Father," Constantine added.

"We must move quickly," Nikolai agreed. "Perhaps plant our own rumors."

"I'll return to the Palace," Constantine offered. "See what can be done."

He crossed to his sister, kissed her briefly on the cheek, nodded to Nikolai, and left. Waiting until the front door slammed shut, Nikolai took Katria back into his arms. She felt slight against him, though he knew her to be strong in so many ways.

"I don't want you to worry," he said, "I'll find a way to manage the situation."

"You're not alone in this, Nikolai." Her arms tightened around his back, though she didn't move. She cleared her throat, and for an instant he worried she was crying. But no, not his Katria. She was angry, calculating again.

"And I *am* concerned. I understand just as well as anyone what disfavor among the court can do."

He knew her words to be true, and didn't wish to dispute them simply for the sake of doing so. A hint of a smile played around his mouth.

She was a strong woman, his Katria. He wished he could have seen her in court when confronted with these rumors. Not to see her defend him, but to see her anger; she was so beautiful when she was angry.

"I shall speak to the tsar directly." He didn't want her worrying—*concerning* herself—about things neither could control. It was in Fate's hands now, and all any of them could do was wait to see what their maneuvers wrought. "As it stands, it's all rumor and conjecture."

"Nikolai, that's all it takes," she snapped.

He wondered if that was truly worry, or more of her anger. No, he thought, watching her eyes flick between his, it was worry. She could lie all she wanted, but to him, her eyes told the truth.

"Or have you been out of the country too long?" she added.

His eyes narrowed, but she plunged on.

"They'll envelop you in the conjecture. In the lies. They'll tear bits off you until nothing is left. We'll have to act quickly and decisively." Her eyes shone vividly with her anger, her luscious mouth pressed into a tight line. "I'm resolved to see you're no longer torn apart by those vipers."

"Since I met you, I've admired that resolve." He held her waist, pulling her close. When she started to move away, he grabbed her tightly to him. "I don't want you between me and my enemies."

"I'm already there," she replied. "And I intend to use *my* position to *your* advantage."

"I won't allow—"

Her mouth was hot on his, knocking whatever he planned to say from his mind. Sensual and eager, the vaulted control she held over her emotions erupted. When she pulled back, looking defiantly at him, he was lost.

Wrenching her into his arms, he kissed her. Katria consumed him, drowning out all but her. Nikolai breathed in the scent of her, heard her moan. Deepening the kiss, he seized this chance. Her arms wound around his neck, her body pressed close to his.

Breaking the kiss, he rested his forehead against hers. He shouldn't have done that. Even barely touching her, he could taste her. Wanted her. He could envision her on his bed, spread before him. Cursing his weakness, he dropped his hands and took a step back.

"What's wrong?"

"I want you now even more than before." The words felt torn from him, honesty ringing in the rough admission.

He saw the change in her immediately. Whereas before, Katria would've laughed it off or taken a step backwards, now she stepped forward. Arousal blasted through him. She smiled up at him, one soft hand cupping his cheek. Curling his own hands into fists, Nikolai swallowed hard.

"I want you as well." Her words were strong in the silence. "And I don't see a reason why we should wait any longer."

It was the surrender he desired.

"I still intend to have you in my bed every night."

So saying, he kissed her. He couldn't describe the kiss. It was physically deeper though it was no more than a kiss. The power of the emotion behind both her response and his reaction to it surprised him and made him want more. There was a twinge of sadness, of frustration, of concern...*for him*. And so much more, wrapped up in that kiss.

Drawing back, struggling to control himself, Nikolai watched her open her eyes. He saw the depth of her passion in the darkening blue-green. He took her hand and led her out of the study and up the stairs.

Once in his bedroom, Nikolai gently turned her. Kissing along the tops of her shoulders, he undid the long row of buttons hiding her skin from him. With each patch exposed, he tasted the sweetness of her, watched her hands tighten in her skirt. He felt her uneven breathing as she struggled for air. Slowly pushing the material off her shoulders, he trailed his lips along her arm, saw her jump when he kissed the inner elbow.

Scraping his teeth gently over that spot, Nikolai watched her head fall back, her breasts rise and fall. Smiling, he promised himself he'd return to that sensitive area, and slipped a hand behind her head, holding her so he could devour her lips.

"Nikolai," she moaned, opening for him.

No longer tentative when she kissed him, he could taste her own need, the strength of it. She was greedy now, eagerly kissing him back. Sweeping his tongue along her lips, he pushed the dress to the floor, fingers nimble as they untied her underskirts. Lifting her onto the bed, he slid free the knot holding her corset closed.

Breasts spilling from their confines, Katria knelt before him. Her own hands removed corset and chemise to toss them onto the floor with her other clothes.

Nikolai forgot how to breathe.

"Magnificent." Utterly magnificent, naked, she was all he'd imagined and more. *His.*

Holding her breasts, he bent to tease her nipples' already hard peaks. Nipping first one, then the other, he tugged hard and heard her cry. Fearing he'd hurt her, he released the nipple, but before he could move, Katria's hands combed through his hair, pressing him to her breasts.

With a chuckle, he smoothed his tongue around the peak, running his hands down her sides to catch her thighs. Laying her flat on the bed, Nikolai followed her down, kissing over belly and hip, across to the other one.

His fingers found her, felt the heat from her. When he touched her, she arched off the bed, ready for him. He flicked a finger along those most secret of places, slick with need, and she moaned.

With impatient hands, she pushed at his jacket even as her legs wrapped round his hips. Eyes half opened, harsh breathing pressing her all-too-tempting breasts against his chest, he snapped.

Nikolai planned to take the rest of the afternoon to know her, to learn the secrets of her body, to watch her shatter with passion. To claim her and posses her. Standing straight, fingers fumbling with his waist-coat and shirt buttons, he forgot all that. He forgot everything save the passion between them, the insistent need.

His shoes gave him trouble, but when Katria sat up, kissed his shoulder, and ran her hand along his spine, he ripped them off and quickly shed his pants.

He had to have her now.

The half smile on her face turned minx-like when she saw him. Grabbing her hips, he tugged her down, crushed his lips to hers, spread her open for him. Entwining their hands, he raised her arms over her head, watching her.

"Nikolai," she whimpered, restless.

In one hard thrust, he was buried inside her. Heaven. Nothing in his existence prepared him for what it felt like to be buried in her warmth. She cried out and moved slightly beneath him. Releasing one of her hands, he tweaked her nipple, rolling it between his fingers. His mouth was gentle on hers while he waited for her to adjust to him. To respond again.

She released the breath she'd held, relaxed and moved her hips against his. Taking his cue, Nikolai withdrew only to drive back deeper. Katria's hips rose to meet his, tentative at first, then winding her legs around his waist. He felt the change in her as he moved, as she met him with each thrust. Lost, knowing only her, nothing else mattered save her pleasure and his.

Finding her nub, he rubbed it. She exploded beneath him, crying out, tightening around him. Releasing the tight control he'd held over himself, Nikolai thrust once, twice, the sheer power of his release catching him unawares and ripping violently through him.

His arms gave out, and he rolled to the side, instantly gathering Katria to him.

****

Crumpling the note, Sergey let loose a pleased laugh. He strode to the doors and shouted for his son. The moment Pavel entered the study, he raised his glass of vodka.

"We've won." He toasted. Laughing again, he generously poured a glass for Pavel.

"Markova agreed?"

Another rich laugh reverberated along the walls. "I knew he cared more for his family's position than anything. That bastard would marry off his mad wife to gain status."

Pavel knocked back his drink, unsurprisingly pouring another. "So Mikhail gets the Markova woman. *Hmph.*"

Sergey looked at his younger son, dismissing his disappointment in the grander scheme of the Radoff family. Both his sons disappointed him, though Pavel was by far the most like him in cunning and astuteness. His younger son's weakness was drink and his violent sexual tendencies. Those could be overlooked when compared with Mikhail's weakness—his complete disregard for family, his love of Russia, his *honesty.* Oh, the boy could play the political game as well as any Russian, but he lacked the talent for deception that went on behind closed doors, the ingenuity needed to procure status, power, and wealth.

With a disappointed sigh he refused to let spoil his current mood, Sergey wondered if one of his younger daughters would follow in his steps. There was always hope.

"At the very least," Pavel continued, eyeing the decanter, "she'll be part of the family." His grin widened as he looked at Sergey. "In this house—where I'll have access to her any time."

Scowling, his mood close to being ruined, Sergey reminded himself of the lands and money Katria Markova would bring with her marriage. The strip of fertile land bordering his eastern estates was particularly key. It would give him ownership of nearly the entire region along the Dnepr River.

In truth, he wouldn't have cared who Mikhail married, so long as the woman boasted a handsome inheritance and connections in government. And there was a small part of him, a very small part, that did want grandchildren. The Radoff name needed to survive, and Sergey couldn't count on Pavel keeping a healthy wife long enough to conceive a child.

Determined not to let his sons spoil his mood, Sergey poured another drink and laughed again. "Inform your brother of the happy news," he instructed.

****

Katria smiled over her shoulder at Nikolai's bent head. "I thought you'd have more experience with a woman's buttons."

His teeth nipped her shoulder, and she shivered in reaction. Her skin was sensitive to the touch, and Nikolai touched her everywhere. His hands were slow as they slipped her chemise over her head, tied her corset, and rebuttoned the dozens of buttons lining her gown. And his mouth was everywhere.

Dear God, she'd never expected losing her virginity could feel so—delicious. Wicked. She felt insatiable, wanted to feel him again. Reveling in the wantonness, understanding the power Nikolai held over her, the pull of his desires, Katria turned.

She wound her arms about his neck, and stood on tiptoes to kiss him. Letting the feel of his kisses wash through her, drug her, she wanted to feel his skin under her fingertips, undress and explore him as he had her.

"I understand you so much better now than when we first met," she admitted.

"You were wary of me at first," he said against her mouth.

"I was." She pulled back just enough to look at him. "I didn't quite appreciate the reasons behind"—she floundered for a heartbeat but settled for—"the attentions you paid me. But now I do, and I share in them."

He growled, mouth hard on hers. This possession thrilled her as it once unnerved her. Accepting it, she let the kiss spiral out of control, desperate to have more. When she leaned forward, forgetting all save him, Nikolai pulled back. Holding her at arm's length, he struggled to breathe.

Katria smiled, pleased with his reaction, with the control *she* held over *him*. "I don't want to leave this house, leave your arms, but I'm... concerned."

His fingers combed through her hair, which was loose now, and gently trailed over her cheek, down her arms to entwine with her own. "Not of the rumors?" His voice was harsh, eyes serious. "Surely you're not afraid of what those at court say?"

Abruptly, Katria realized the answer to a question she'd had days ago. Yes. He would fight for her.

"No..." She shook her head and tried to put her fear into words. "We can't lock ourselves here forever. The world will interfere. It will find us."

As if in answer to her fears, a commotion echoed from below. Nikolai released her hands, racing for the door. Dread settled in the pit of her stomach, and Katria ran after him. Among the raised voices from the foyer, she heard one strident voice over all the rest.

Viktor.

Stumbling on the stairs, she reached for the railing, gripping it with whitened knuckles to steady herself. It was no use. She had to continue on. Her father obviously knew she was here; to hide would be futile. Closing her eyes, drawing in a deep breath, Katria prepared to continue down when she heard the unmistakable sounds of fist hitting flesh.

"Where is she?" her father screamed.

Rounding the curve in the stairs, Katria saw two burly men—hired by her father, no doubt—holding Nikolai's arms behind his back as a third hired man punched him.

"Search everywhere!" Viktor shouted. "Secure the house!"

"Nikolai!" she screamed, flying down the final steps, stepping between the man hitting her lover and Nikolai. "Stop it!" she shouted.

But her hands were ineffectual on the men's grip. Her father paid them far too well for them to stop at a woman's cries.

Rage such as she'd never felt before enveloped her, and she tried to see if Nikolai was all right. His mouth was bloodied, but he watched her silently, black eyes immutable. Instinctively she knew he hadn't said a word. No, he wouldn't have. He'd take the beating and try to find her before her father did—hide her, keep her safe.

A hard hand yanked her from Nikolai.

"What disgrace is this?" Viktor demanded. "You dishonor all of us."

"Father, we're to be married!" Before she could say more, he smacked her across mouth and she stumbled backwards.

Nikolai roared. She could feel the force of his anger even through her shock. Eyes watering from the slap, she watched him throw off one of the men, but her father had thought ahead. She'd only seen the three attacking her Nikolai, but two more emerged from the flickering shadows to restrain him.

Through the din, her father loomed over her. "No, you are not." He grabbed her wrist, yanking her upright. "I'll not allow you to marry into this traitorous family."

"Coward!" she spat defiantly. With her free hand, she swung at him. Her palm met his cheek, infuriating him further. "Your actions are foolish. It's still to your advantage to retain your connections to the Orlovs."

Another of his hired men pulled her arms behind her back, steering her toward the door. On the floor, she could see Lev, Nikolai's butler, blood around his temple, unmoving. She could hear Nikolai's growls and knew he was outmatched. She tried to turn, but couldn't see around the guard's massive body.

To Nikolai, Viktor shouted from the door. "The betrothal is off, Orlov. Steer clear of my family."

The guard picked her up and carried her out the door into the frigid winter's evening. The sun had set, blanketing the street in a soft twilight. The carriage she'd left at the Winter Palace waited on the street, the horses snorting softly.

Katria could still hear Nikolai fighting to reach her, but no matter how she struggled, she couldn't so much as cause the giant holding her to grunt. He tossed her into the carriage, and lumbered in after her. Her father sat elegantly across from her, watching her intently.

Glaring at him, she refused to say a word. This wasn't over and they both knew it.

Chapter Seven

MIKHAIL RADOFF wandered through the ever-present crowd of courtiers. It seemed to him the tsar was never afforded peace, never afforded a moment in the Palace when there was no one to vie for his attentions. Even now, Tsar Nicholas hunched near Princess Ulensky, no doubt hearing of the latest scandal.

Nicholas wasn't the type of man to believe every rumor that flitted around these rooms. Mikhail doubted, no matter how vicious Ulensky sounded, that Nicholas would ever move against Orlov without proof. He couldn't afford to. The Orlovs were too powerful, and while Nikolai's uncle, Alexey, ultimately answered to Nicholas, the tsar *was* head of the Third Section.

Yet the Orlovs were the talk of the state rooms. Mikhail wasn't sure how, but he knew his father had been responsible for this contemptible rumor. To accuse a man of treason, stripping him of all honor he had in life, was the worst offense imaginable.

Father, I knew you were capable of much, but this corruption, this scheme is beyond tolerable.

"Mikhail." The elderly Baron Galensky approached, cane tapping steadily on the patterned marble floor. "Such offensive news spreading throughout the room. Have you heard of the circumstances surrounding the death of Peter Orlov?"

"Yes. I've heard the stories." Mikhail scanned the room, full of chattering tongues and spiteful comments. And suddenly, he saw a way out of his impending engagement to Katria. With a sly grin at foiling his father, he told Galensky, "But I would not put any faith in them if I were you."

"Oh?" Galensky's bushy eyebrows raised in question. Despite his years, the old man still knew when to listen and when to disregard the rumors that flowed through court. "Is there some additional news? I heard Peter Orlov was selling military secrets to the Sultan."

"Lies." Mikhail didn't wave a dismissive hand, though he wanted to. He needed Galensky to believe this, not to mistrust another Radoff. "You were acquainted with Alexey's nephew. Do you truly believe him the type of man to betray Russia? No." He shook his head adamantly. "I've heard it's all lies spread by enemies of the Orlovs. With Alexey Orlov out of Russia, and Nikolai just returned a short while ago, they are vulnerable to this type of manipulation."

Galensky stared at him for a bit, and Mikhail wondered if he'd been too blasé. But then the other man nodded. "I supposed that's quite true."

"Yes." He bowed to the Baron. "If you'll excuse me."

He left Galensky to spread his own rumor, and went to find Anna Tiomkin. While it was most likely too late, he wanted her to hear about his marriage to Katria from him. He wanted her to know he was a better man than his father, and he wanted to spread the rumor he'd just begun about the Orlovs. Not that many would believe the closest friend of Katria Markova, but if his name were attached to it….

Grinning, he cut through the crowd, intent on his search. There. Anna stood in a group of women, listening with a thoughtful look on her face. She said little, he noticed, but her eyes focused on each individual speaker in turn. One of the finest beauties in court, he'd long been attracted to her. While Mikhail knew she was interested in marrying him, he wasn't certain he could subject her to a life with his father. Or worse, to Pavel's attentions.

Now that Katria was promised to him, Mikhail realized the depth of his feelings toward Anna, and regretted not offering for her sooner.

Bowing to the group in general, he held out his arm to Anna. "If you'll excuse us," he said, smiling, "I wish to speak with Countess Tiomkin."

Amongst the tittering, he led her slowly along the perimeter of the room. Anna walked silently beside him, and he knew he was too late. She'd heard.

"It wasn't my doing, Anna," he said softly, "but I hope to rectify it soon."

When she looked up at him, her blue eyes shimmered with hope.

"I told Baron Galensky I didn't believe a word about the Orlovs," he said, and saw she looked confused. "And implied he may use my name attached to this rumor."

"Mikhail," she said, stopping to turn to him. Her hand was urgent in his, and he wondered if she knew how intimate they looked. "Your father will be furious!"

"I don't care, Anna," he said, squeezing her hand before continuing their walk. "I don't want to spend my life following the orders of that… man. With luck, this will allow Nikolai to resume his engagement to Katria."

"You're right," she breathed. "It is just a rumor. There's no evidence, and the tsar doesn't take it seriously."

They walked for a time in silence, and he was very aware of the stares that followed them. This was the first time they'd been so public in their affections. Despite everything, he found he didn't mind.

"Mikhail…" She trailed off, and he wondered what she wanted to say. But Anna shook her head and lapsed back into silence.

"I'll be free of Father soon enough, Anna," he assured her. Then he admitted aloud for the first time, "It's you I want."

Anna tripped to a stop, and Mikhail couldn't help but smile. It was oddly freeing to admit such a thing, to know his plans for the future were coalescing.

****

"Whore!"

Viktor pushed her into the room, glaring as she stumbled over an ottoman. Katria pulled herself up. Oh, how she wanted to kill him. If she could with her bare hands, she'd do so tonight. As it was, she refused to let him intimidate her. This was the reason she'd become as hard as she had; as a way to survive Viktor Markova.

Calling on all her control, she fought back fear for Nikolai—she didn't even know if he lived—and faced her father.

"Don't think simply because you chose to ruin yourself with that traitor that it changes anything!" Viktor's voice shook the room, but she didn't let that sway her.

"He isn't a traitor, Father," she shouted back. "There's no shred of proof! This scandal will pass." She paused. Regaining her composure, she regretted calling him a coward. Oh, she meant it, but with that one sentence, she lost much of her power. "I believe in him."

In quick strides, Viktor crossed the room, grabbed her upper arms, and slammed her against the wall. The wind knocked out of her, her head aching, Katria struggled to bring her father's menacing features into focus.

"I don't care what you believe." He brought his face close to hers, and his voice lowered further, if that was possible. "You are not to have a thought I do not give you." He shook her again, banging her once more against the wall. Pain exploded behind her eyes, but she didn't cry out. "You are an instrument for this family. Since your birth, I've had only one use for you—a marriage for the advancement of our name and wealth."

Another shake, and no matter how she tried to prepare herself, Katria couldn't prevent her head from slamming back against the wall. "I will not have you threaten our name by continuing to associate with Orlov."

Head spinning, pounding, Katria snarled at him. "I threaten nothing being with Nikolai."

Viktor sneered at her—she saw that clearly enough through the haze of pain—and yanked her forward, only to slam her one last time against the plaster wall. The absurd thought that the plaster cracked had her wondering how he'd explain it to the work men, but then he released her. Knees unable to sustain her, Katria dropped to the ground.

Show no weakness, she chanted inwardly. *Show no weakness.*

"You will do whatever it is women do to show you are pure on your wedding night," he said.

Katria glared, unable to hide her hatred of him any longer. To her surprise, Viktor laughed. She watched him turn away, but he went no more than a step before he spun on his heel and kicked her. Lying on the floor, struggling to breathe, Katria thanked Nikolai for fully dressing her. The boned corset saved her from serious harm, she was certain.

Her father's footsteps echoed along the marble foyer and down the hall. Only then did she uncurl her fists from her skirt and slide herself upright, using the wall for support. Katria looked down at her gown; it was wrinkled from her earlier activities. Had it been such a short time ago? So much had happened this day, yet even now she could recall with crystalline clarity the feel of Nikolai's touch.

With an unsteady hand, she probed the tender back of her head. As she suspected, bits of plaster fell away, but she saw only a small amount of blood. Unwilling to call a servant, Katria crawled to a chair and stood. Her knees wobbled, and she wasn't sure her legs could carry her up to her room.

As carefully as she could, she walked out of the parlor and toward the stairs. The last thing she remembered was Nikolai's face, furiously glaring at Viktor, when she'd raced down his townhouse stairs to stop the attack of her father's guards.

"Please be alive," she whispered before her steely will could no longer support her, and darkness enveloped her.

****

February 14, 1855
Georgian Calendar

Nikolai snarled at those bold enough to stare. It hurt to breathe, and while Markova's damned *Tatars* had been careful not to hit his face, they weren't that careful. His lips were bruised, and even snarling hurt. His servants tried to bandage him the best they could, but no amount of vodka dulled the ache. He'd barely been conscious when Constantine had arrived later that night.

Through it all, he saw Katria's frantic face and heard her struggles to break free from her father. He'd wanted to go to her immediately, but when he'd tried to stand, his legs betrayed him. Face down on the floor, Nikolai attempted to breathe through the pain as Constantine helped him back to the bed and promised to check on Katria. That did little to allay Nikolai's fears.

His friend reported that while Viktor had threatened her, she was in perfect health. The tone of his voice had Nikolai wondering, but Constantine insisted all was well with her. Save for the fact she was confined to her rooms, locked in the castle tower, as it were. Making Constantine swear to watch over her until he could get to her himself, Nikolai collapsed.

When he woke the next day, he had a new plan. There was little doubt the tsar had already heard the rumors surrounding Nikolai and Peter. As the papers found on Peter had yet to surface, Nikolai knew the bribes he had paid out proved useful. It was a simple matter of speaking with the tsar.

And keeping an eye on Lazarenko and Terenov.

It wasn't difficult to find Nicholas. The state rooms were half empty, so Nikolai followed the long line of people to where the tsar held court. He wasn't surprised the masses parted for him, but he *was* surprised when Nicholas wordlessly gestured to a private salon.

"Your Imperial Majesty." Nikolai bowed.

"Orlov." The tsar nodded.

Nikolai began his well-rehearsed speech. He'd had nothing but time these last few days to plan this move. "There have been stories about my brother's death. I've come to assure you they're not true. I'm unclear as to what Peter worked on at the time of his death, but know it was in the defense of you and Russia. I spent time with him abroad, and know all he did—"

"Enough!" Nicholas raised a forestalling hand. "Enough. Your defense of your brother is unnecessary. I have full faith in your Uncle Alexey, as I did in Peter. Until I see proof to the contrary, I will not engage in idle gossip."

Nikolai nodded his thanks, was about to pursue the matter of his marriage to Katria when the tsar surprised him.

"I see you've been out of court for several days." Nicholas's bejeweled hand waved in the general direction of Nikolai's face, but he was too polite to say anything about the bruises. "There are other rumors, that enemies of the Orlovs spread lies about both Peter and you."

Constantine worked quickly, Nikolai thought. Then, before Nicholas could leave, he apologized. "I do have one more matter, Your Imperial Majesty." Nicholas nodded, waiting more patiently than Nikolai expected. "That of the approval for my wedding to Countess Katria Markova."

The look the tsar gave him told Nikolai that Markova hadn't officially announced Katria's new betrothal, but those rumors had also spread.

"Nikolai," the tsar said quietly, and he sensed some sympathy in his emperor's voice. "I gave my approval, but her father's approval takes precedence. Now." He clasped his hands behind his back, puffing his chest out so the medals on his dark blue military uniform bounced in the gas-lighted room. "If you'll excuse me, Orlov, I have matters of war to attend to."

Bowing as the tsar left, Nikolai cursed Viktor Markova, and vowed to get Katria back.

Stalking through the state rooms, ignoring the looks and whispers, he worried for her. Despite Constantine's assurances and his repeated visits to Nikolai, the fact that he himself could not see Katria, could not get to her through the guards her damned father placed around the townhouse, had Nikolai on the edge of panic.

Guilt sliced through him. He should have had more control when it came to her. For months, he'd waited for her to come around, to see him for who he was and not cringe whenever he touched her. Or pull away to hide behind her emotional wall.

He could still taste her, feel her beneath him. He wanted her again, wasn't certain he'd ever tire of—

"Count Orlov!"

Nikolai turned at the summons, surprised anyone had the courage to directly confront him. Countess Anna Tiomkin rushed across the top of the Jordan staircase. Breathless, she looked around, though both of them knew total privacy was near impossible.

"I spoke with Katria," she whispered. "She wishes me to tell you she misses you."

Nikolai tried to discern the truth of her words. He knew Katria considered Countess Tiomkin her closest friend, but with the capricious flick of Fate's hand, he trusted only Constantine and Katria.

"Is she well?" he demanded.

With a hesitant nod, Anna said, "Yes. She's well. Her father forbids her from coming to the Palace or venturing out these days. I'm closely supervised when visiting. It's my understanding she'll receive Mikhail Radoff tomorrow."

Seeing red, Nikolai barely refrained from shaking the woman. She meant well, he knew, but her news did little to appease him. He'd kill Radoff—the whole damned family!

"Please get word to her," he managed in a civil enough tone, "and tell her I'll find a way."

****

Constantine snarled at the guard and ordered him out of the room. He'd purposely dressed in all his medals and ribbons, and it seemed the military attire of the tsar's Imperial Guards intimidated the hired peasants Viktor now kept around the house.

Katria stood before him in a deep blue dressing gown, looking far better than she had yesterday morning when he'd last seen her. A bowl of melting snow sat on the wash table, a wet cloth beside it, and he cursed his father again. He'd murder the old bastard for what he did to Katria.

"Your color has improved," Constantine said, feeling awkward standing there.

"I'm feeling better." She smiled, and he could see it didn't pain her as it had. She reached a hand out and drew him to the window seat. "Not as sore, and the room spins less." She paused, and he knew her question. "Have you seen Nikolai? Is he all right?"

"I haven't seen him since two days past, but he's much improved," Constantine said. He omitted the delirious rants Nikolai had as to Viktor's death, Mikhail's torture, and general pain to the rest of the Radoffs.

"I won't marry Mikhail, Constantine," she said seriously. It was the first time she'd mentioned her new betrothal. "I don't care if Father threatens to kill me. I don't care if he does."

"Katria, I'm sorry." Unable to protect her then, unwilling to think about what happened to her these years he'd been away, Constantine hugged her close. "I won't let him touch you again," he swore.

"I know you'll protect me when you're here, Constantine," she said, head tilting on his chest. He wondered if the medals hurt her, but she didn't move. "But you won't always be here. I need to get out of this house and get to Nikolai."

"Katria, I'm trying—"

"It's not that," she reassured him. "I'm afraid what Father will do… what the tsar will do."

"I won't leave you," he promised. "Not until this is resolved and you're married to Nikolai."

They sat like that for some time. He had much to do, both in regard to his military reasons for being in St. Petersburg and to help Nikolai. Yet he held Katria.

"I love you, little sister."

She chuckled and did pull back now. "It's always been us, hasn't it?"

"You had Anatoli," he reminded her. She didn't respond and kissed him on the cheek and rested her head back on his shoulder.

"I love you, too," she whispered. "And I can't wait for this hellish war to end so you can be home again."

"Will you be all right?" he asked. "I need to see Nikolai, but will be back this evening."

"Yes." She nodded. "Father's left me alone since locking me in here."

Constantine kissed the top of her head, reluctant to leave. "I'll see you this eve," he promised.

He hated to leave, but there was much to do before she could be safe and happy. Constantine had known Nikolai for years, but had lost touch when the other man left Russia. He never would have matched him with Katria, but he saw the affection they held for each other. Moreover, he saw the protectiveness Nikolai felt for her. With him, she'd be safe.

He met Viktor on a landing. Grabbing his father by his jacket, he shoved the old man against the wall, rattling the paintings of previous Markovas that lined the staircase.

"I'll be back shortly. Stay away from her. And keep your peasants in the stable where they belong."

The intimidation he saw in Viktor's eyes, the same blue-green his children inherited, flashed briefly and Constantine bared his teeth in a threatening grin. Intimidation was quickly replaced with contempt.

"I'm still the head of this household. I'll do as I wish with my daughter."

"I don't care who you think you are, old man," he snapped. "I'm an officer in the tsar's Imperial Guard and I shall do whatever it takes to protect my sister. Heed my warning." He raised Viktor slightly, only to abruptly drop him. His father staggered. "You'll not get another."

Chapter Eight

February 15, 1855
Georgian Calendar

KATRIA AWAITED Mikhail in the front parlor. A fire roared in the fireplace and the wall where her father had slammed her head was newly repaired and freshly painted. The portrait of her great-grandfather hung over the mantel, staring out at them. His eyes, the same color as hers, were icy as they watched the proceedings of his family.

She wondered now, as the front door opened and their butler showed Mikhail into the house, what Great-Grandfather Constantine would think of the current situation. He would probably approve of her father's every action.

She didn't stand when Mikhail entered.

With an ironic smile, he acknowledged her slight and stood to one side of the settee. He didn't speak first, and with a sigh she relented.

"What is your opinion of all this, Mikhail?" she asked, sweeping her hand to include her, Mikhail, their fathers, Anna, and Nikolai. Especially Nikolai.

Her thoughts were never far from him, though she dared not show even her maid. She worried for him and wanted to see him.

"None of this pleases me, Katria," he admitted. "I know of your feelings for Orlov and guess you know of mine for Anna." She gestured for him to sit, and he nodded in thanks. "Our fathers are making these decisions."

He paused, and she wondered what more there was. She hadn't expected an answer, but at one time she did consider Mikhail Radoff a close acquaintance and felt ignoring him was not the right thing to do.

"I've done what I can," he murmured. "I've spread my own story through court, that Peter's enemies were behind the accusations against him and Nikolai."

"You did?" she asked in wonderment. She assumed it had been Constantine. "I haven't been to the Palace in days," she admitted. "Did they believe you? What do they say about Nikolai?"

"Oh, that was days ago," he laughed. "You know how quickly conversation changes there. Without proof, there's nothing to speak of." Mikhail hesitated, watching her for a heartbeat, then admitted, "I know it was Father who first accused Peter of treason, who spread that first rumor. He's taking advantage of Peter's death and I'm sorry."

"I know you are," she replied. Gratitude flooded her, and she wondered how to ever thank him. "However," she said, as the truth of this meeting crashed around her, "There's still the matter of our marriage. How do we prevent that? How do we change it?"

"I came here to tell you," Mikhail said, standing. She'd never seen him look so proud, so—intent. "I've stayed in Father's house these last days but I have been making arrangements. I plan to break away from Father. I've created a situation which will allow me to ask for Anna's hand."

Katria stood, shocked and pleased. "What is it?"

"I needed to wait for a reply from my mother's brother. He's never cared for Father, and has made me a partner in his shipping business."

"Oh, Mikhail!" Katria threw her arms around him in a quick hug. "That's wonderful news!"

She said nothing about Anna's love of court and St. Petersburg. If Mikhail took this step from under Radoff's roof, Katria knew Anna would follow him anywhere.

Follow him anywhere…

What if she and Nikolai ran away? Before that thought could grow, Mikhail laughed.

The sound so surprised Katria, she let any idea of she and Nikolai go for the moment. She'd never heard Mikhail laugh, not a sound so free, so liberated.

"I wanted to tell you myself," he said, grinning. "Our engagement will not last."

****

He didn't like waiting. Nikolai paced his study as Constantine brought him up to date, but it was no use. No matter how much he cared for his brother, how his family name lay in ruins around him, all he could think of was Katria.

Trapped in that house, he knew she was going to close off from him again. He had to get her out, away from Viktor and into his life. That son-of-a-bitch father of hers would sell her for his own gain.

Worried for her despite both Anna's and Constantine's assurances, he needed to see her for himself. He wanted to hold her. His body ached for her, and at night, he found himself waking to search the bed for her.

"Talk against Peter has significantly died down these last few days," Constantine was saying. "And I've managed to do some reconnaissance work for you."

"Yes?" Nikolai forced his mind to focus on Constantine's words.

"Terenov's name has arisen on more than one occasion. We'll need to watch him."

Nikolai's eyes narrowed. "Terenov has been well compensated for his trouble. Too well compensated, if even a hint of this has leaked out."

"He's been ever present," Constantine said, pouring himself another splash of vodka.

Nikolai was surprised; his friend didn't usually drink when matters this important arose. Was it that Constantine had too much to do with helping him, keeping an eye on Katria, and his own military orders? Or was it the matter at hand—treason and the Radoffs?

Lev, his butler, interrupted him with a discreet cough. "Excellency," he said and bowed. "The footman has returned."

Nikolai smiled and gestured for the man to be brought in. Constantine joined him, but didn't ask questions.

"He goes by the name Wowk," the footman said quickly. He looked cold, but Nikolai didn't bother offering a glass of vodka. He compensated the man handsomely. "I followed him for three nights, and he stays at The Boar by the Neva, near the Admiralty."

"Good. The others?"

"They drink together, but don't sleep in The Boar."

Dismissing him, Nikolai turned back to Constantine. He'd take care of the men guarding Markova's house tonight. "Is there more about Peter?"

Constantine resumed his stance beside the fireplace. "I also heard the tsar used Peter's death to his advantage."

"How so?" Nikolai demanded.

"Nicholas managed to reestablish a lost connection." Constantine shrugged. "I'm not privy to all the details."

"Anatoli might know," he said, and Constantine nodded. "I'll contact him."

Pacing to the windows, Nikolai opened a curtain to look out. The street did little to inspire him, but the monotony of twilight served to center his thoughts. He thought he saw Katria cross the street. His heart leapt, but he knew the woman wasn't her.

Never far from his mind, he easily envisioned Katria's warm body beneath his, heard her moan his name. All thoughts of the tsar and any plot the other man had just disappeared. Shaking his head, Nikolai let the curtain drop.

What had Nicholas gained by Peter's death? More, what did the tsar gain by prolonging these rumors?

"If the tsar had something to do with the accident," Nikolai said slowly, "there's nothing I can do."

"And if it wasn't him?" Constantine asked.

He slowly turned toward the other man. "I'll destroy whoever's behind this."

****

Dismounting, Nikolai followed the footman through the shadows. He could hear the roar of drunken peasants though the open windows, smell the stench of unwashed bodies despite the winds rushing down the street. Brightly lighted with gas lamps perched precariously along the walls, the room was filled to bursting.

"The one by the fire." His footman pointed.

Wowk was as burly as Nikolai remembered, though he couldn't be certain this was the hired man who held him down. The memory was blurry except for Katria's struggles. "Wait by the horses," he ordered.

Opening the door, Nikolai allowed his eyes to adjust to the brightness. The din decreased as he moved into the room, a well-dressed gentleman among working men. Stopping before Wowk's table, he waited for the brute to notice him.

"You work for Markova." It wasn't a question.

Wowk jerked in surprise. Without waiting for more, he pulled a knife, knocking the stool back as he stood.

Off guard, Nikolai jumped, avoiding the stab. This was the man, then. He knew there'd be retribution. Grabbing Wowk's knife arm, he quickly twisted it behind his back before Wowk's free arm, looking roughly the size of a tree and being propelled toward his face, had the chance to hit him.

Wowk cried out and went to his knees. Taking the knife from Wowk's limp fingers, even as the bigger man lashed out, Nikolai stabbed him. Wowk fell backwards.

"Anyone else in Markova's employ?" No one answered. Not that Nikolai expected them to. "Don't be." He tilted his head to the dead Wowk. "That's what happens to those who work for Markova."

Exiting the dead-quiet tavern, he returned to the footman and his horse. Markova was less of a threat now.

****

February 14, 1855
Georgian Calendar

Katria stepped from the house wrapped in her sable-trimmed cloak. She took Constantine's arm as they descended the steps to the waiting carriage and nervously smoothed her red broadcloth gown. In honor of her brother's powers of persuasion, she wore a gown modeled after the uniforms of the Imperial Guards.

"Where are the guards?" she asked. Knowing Viktor as she did, Katria doubted he'd have simply dismissed them until she was safely delivered to Mikhail and well on her way to having a child.

Constantine's eyes glittered. "Ask Nikolai."

He hadn't abandoned her. With her brother's words, Katria's heart warmed. Nikolai hadn't abandoned her, but had disposed of Viktor's guards to get to her. Smiling, she waited while the butler opened the door.

How Constantine managed to convince their father to release her from her room, let alone the house, Katria didn't know and

Constantine didn't say. Thrilled to leave behind the bedroom she once loved, she'd have gone anywhere.

As it was, she knew they drove toward Nikolai's. Anxious to see him again, yet anticipating the meeting far too much, she was restless as they moved through town.

"Relax, Katria," Constantine laughed.

"I'll calm when I see Nikolai." But she did still her hands and smile at her brother.

In the days since she'd last seen him, Katria wavered between knowing he cared for her and wondering if he no longer wanted her. His actions after they made love told her one thing, but the way she was pulled from his arms, the fact she hadn't seen him since, left her doubting her own certainty.

If Viktor hadn't held her prisoner for days, Katria knew these feelings would be long resolved. As it was, this was the first opportunity she had to see Nikolai.

Hating that anxiety, knowing he still wanted to marry her, Katria tried to calm herself. Alas, it was of little use. The carriage eventually pulled to a stop in front of his house, and the nerves she worked so hard to calm on the ride there made themselves known.

Constantine helped her out and hurried her up the walkway to the already-opened door. Just beyond, Nikolai stood. Unthinking, Katria rushed into his arms.

Nikolai's lips were hard on hers, but his hands were gentle as they cupped her face and held her close. Feeling as if she drowned in the currents between them, Katria kissed him back, all her fears dissolved.

"I missed you," she murmured when she could draw breath.

"Are you all right?" he demanded, holding her from him to scrutinize her face. "Did that son of a bitch hurt you?"

"No, no," she whispered. "I'm fine."

"Good." He kissed her again, lifting her against him to carry her up the stairs to his bedroom.

Lost in his arms, in his kiss, in the knowledge he wanted her just as much as he always had, Katria knew why she feared losing him. He was the only person she had every trusted besides Constantine and Anna. Though she respected and admired Anatoli, she hid things from him as well.

Nikolai set her on the chair before the fire and knelt before her. His hands rubbed her arms beneath her cloak.

"You're sure?"

"Yes," she managed. Shaking her head and chuckling, she leaned forward to kiss him again. "No matter what happens," she promised, "I won't doubt."

"Doubt?" he asked, fingers tightening on hers. "Doubt what?"

"Nothing." She took a deep breath and ran her fingers through his hair, feeling absurdly giddy. "I spoke with Mikhail," she said.

He growled. "I'll kill him if he's touched you."

"No!" she said quickly. "No, I promise you, no." Kissing him again because she could, because she wanted to, Katria reveled in the heat that flowed through her, in wanting him as she did.

"No," she repeated, breathing heavy when she pulled back. If they didn't stop, she'd never tell him of Mikhail's visit and she was certain her education in the sexual arts would continue. Shuddering in pleasure at the thought of Nikolai naked, atop her, within her, touching her, Katria purposefully pushed him back and stood.

She needed distance for this, and he was too much of a distraction. "Mikhail—"

"I don't want to hear about Mikhail," he said.

Nikolai's voice was low and dangerous, his eyes hot, black coals boring into her. Katria's heart pounded and her breath caught as her blood sped through her. *Mikhail? Who?*

Pulling her off her feet, Nikolai's mouth crushed hers. He didn't give her room to maneuver, or breath to protest, or time to think. Not that she minded. Her hands clawed the buttons of his shirt, desperate to feel his skin. Finally feeling his hard chest under her questing hands,

Katria sighed, wanting to taste him but too addicted to his mouth to stop.

When Nikolai turned her around, his mouth hot along her neck, across her shoulders, she didn't think. Couldn't. Her gown pooled to the floor, the petticoats quickly following. He spun her again, lifting her to the bed, kissing her. Katria felt something rip, but didn't care as cool air suddenly caressed her flushed skin a moment before Nikolai broke the kiss, his mouth leaving a hot trail down her throat, across the tops of her breasts now unbound by her corset.

Thoughts muddled, all she knew was him: the taste, the feel, the scent. All she wanted was him. His mouth closed over her nipple, sucking on the engorged point, and Katria cried out his name. "Nikolai!"

He moved to her other breast, his strong arms still holding her upright. Hands fisted in his hair and she rocked against him, urging him to continue. She'd never felt like this, so unrestrained, so open. So free. She couldn't begin to fathom the need that sprang from deep within, and didn't bother to try.

They crashed backwards onto the bed. Her teeth nipped his shoulder, tongue tasting flesh, fingertips exploring his back. She wanted more, to taste him from head to toe as he had tasted her, to watch him explode and know she'd been the cause. Nikolai grasped her hands, holding them above her, and gazed down.

"Perfect," he murmured.

She wanted to say something, but words escaped her. Katria leaned up, closing the distance between them, desperate to quench the fire she ignited, to feel him within her. But he wouldn't be rushed. Releasing her hands, his own smoothed up her stomach, over her hips, to her breasts, as his mouth found the opening of her desire, and he tasted her. This was new; this was different.

Even with her limited knowledge of sex, Katria could tell things had changed. Or maybe *she* had.

Nikolai's tongue flicked over her belly, moved lower. Katria stopped breathing. Surely he wouldn't? Her hands gripped his head and tried to pull him up. She felt the laugh along her skin, shuddering through her as longing overrode sense and his tongue found her most intimate secrets.

"Oh, my," she managed.

His hands gripped her thighs, spreading them wide for him. Every movement raced along her nerves, bringing her closer to the peak she craved. His tongue circled the point of her pleasure, teasing. She bucked against him, but he held her still.

Hands clutching the sheets of his bed, Katria tried to move; she wanted more. Then she whimpered in protest as he left her center, pushing her legs into the mattress, moving lips over hip and belly.

Suddenly he leaned forward, his body draped over hers.

"Katria," he said, voice strained. "Look at me." His voice was soft and gentle, yet demanding; ragged with desire, need, and want.

She couldn't resist. Wild with yearning, desperate for more, for all of him, she locked her gaze with his. There was something within his gaze she couldn't make out.

Finding the button of his pants, she quickly undid it with trembling fingers, shoved them down as far as she could reach. He was naked, gloriously naked before her. Katria shuddered. Her body hummed from his touch, begged him for more.

When he entered her, Katria cried out. She moved her hips, rolled them against his, but he paused. Restless, her hands moved up his chest, and her nails scraped down his back, leaving long welts along the way as she clutched him closer against her.

"Please," she moaned.

"Look at me," Nikolai growled. The sound vibrated along her skin, and Katria thought she could grow to love it.

Struggling to open her eyes, Katria wrapped her legs around his waist. She gasped as he slid deeper into her. He set a hard, fast pace, though his mouth moving along her skin was gentle. His fingers found her again, stroking her nub.

Katria shattered. Waves of pure pleasure crashed through her, blanking her mind, blinding her to everything save desire and Nikolai. His name fell from her lips, then nothing.

Nikolai moved again and the delicious sensation of him doing so stirred her. He thrust once, twice, face buried in her shoulder.

"Katria."

He collapsed atop her, and she held him close. Unwilling to move, to let him go, Katria drifted to sleep, utterly sated.

****

Whistling as he opened the door, his last night in his family townhouse, Mikhail stepped inside. Instantly, he quieted. These past several days, as Sergey planned his latest scheme—and Mikhail's wedding to Katria—the house had an air of festivity Mikhail never expected. Now, the mood of the house felt oppressive.

He wondered, as he removed his gloves and hat and handed the butler his walking stick and overcoat, if it was his imagination.

Stepping into the parlor, he saw his father beside the mantel. Not an unusual occurrence, Sergey standing there with glass of liquor in his hand, but something about this scene made Mikhail wish he hadn't returned. He started for the stairs; he'd have to pack quietly, take only the necessities.

"Mikhail!" Sergey bellowed. "Come here. I wish to speak with you."

"What is it, Father?" Mikhail barely hid his contempt. "I'm expected back at the Palace this evening."

"Are you now?" Sergey gestured for his son to move further into the room. "Unless the tsar has summoned you personally, I'm certain you can make time for your Father."

Offering Sergey a shrug, he waited near one of the quilted leather chairs dotting his father's office.

"You've been extremely busy haven't you, Mikhail?"

"I've been meeting with my new fiancé—"

"And spreading rumors at court, rumors that involve enemies of the Orlovs?" Sergey threw his glass at Mikhail.

His hand on his chest where the glass bounced, Mikhail brushed off the pungent liquor. Anything he truly needed, he'd send a servant for. He should have done this years ago, but hadn't a reason until now. *Anna.* Fully intending to marry her, Mikhail wondered if she'd run away with him or if he'd have to find new lodgings in St. Petersburg for the time being.

"And what of the letters I found today?" Sergey demanded from behind him.

Turning slowly to face his father, Mikhail stood his ground. "I'm leaving, Father. I have no intention of marrying Katria nor of remaining in this house for another night."

"I'm still head of this family," Sergey shouted. "You'll do as I say!"

"No, Father," Mikhail said, not bothering to turn. "I won't. Disown me, curse my name, do what you will. I care no more."

There were plenty of lodgings he could rent despite his newly diminished finances, he thought as he buttoned his coat and pulled on his gloves. Sergey threw another glass against the wall, but Mikhail ignored it. Once he'd have surrendered his desires, resigned to whatever his father ordered.

He didn't wait for the butler, who stood there looking both awed and angry at his final leaving, to open the door. Yanking it open, he breathed in the cold air.

He'd break the engagement between him and Katria, make his intentions known to Anna and—

Pain exploded through his skull, and Mikhail dropped to his knees. His last sight was the snow-covered hedges. His last thought was of Anna.

****

"You dare do this to me?" Sergey growled. "Weak, insolent child!"

Bringing the walking stick down again on his son's head, he straightened. Breathing deeply, he smoothed back his hair, tugged at the sleeves of his shirt, straightened the tips of his tie. But when he looked down at the boy, this weak child of his, any attempt at restraint vanished.

"Look at the mess you have caused!" Taking out a handkerchief, he wiped the splatters of blood off the silver handle. He kicked the boy, then reined in his temper. Mikhail didn't move. Good. "You'll not cause problems for this family any longer."

Sweeping his gaze over the vacant street, Sergey stepped back inside. To the butler, he said, "My son suffered a seizure. Bring him up stairs and call the doctor."

Without looking at the man doing his bidding, Sergey examined his walking stick. "And bring me a new cane," he commanded, tossing it at the butler. "This one is ruined."

Chapter Nine

February 16, 1855
Georgian Calendar

THE DOOR cracked open. Katria frowned and pushed it, revealing the dim interior of her friend's bedroom. Anna sat on the window seat, the heavy curtains pulled back only enough to reveal a sliver of wintry afternoon sunlight.

"Anna?" Sitting beside her, Katria took her friend's hands.

"I thought I could love him." The voice was so quiet, so soft, Katria wondered if she'd imagined it.

"Oh, Anna," she sighed, pulling the other woman into her arms. "Be strong, darling."

On the carriage ride here, she'd debated telling Anna of Mikhail's plans. Not only did she not know whether Mikhail had told her what he planned, but she hadn't been certain of Anna's feelings. Infatuation was one thing, love something else entirely.

Her own relief at not having to marry Mikhail was tempered with sadness at a friend's death. And with sympathy for Anna's misery.

"I know of your feelings toward Mikhail," Katria continued. "But circumstances were not in your favor."

"I know, Katria," she whispered, voice cracking. "But I had hope."

Nodding, Katria remained silent. She didn't know what to say that wouldn't sound trite, and had no wish to grieve Anna further with useless knowledge about Mikhail's wish to marry her. Maybe someday, but certainly not now.

****

Viktor watched Sergey Radoff stand before him, perfectly poised, looking as if he just returned from vacationing on the Black Sea, not from burying his eldest son. He offered the other man a glass of vodka, which Sergey accepted with a nod.

It was no secret why Radoff called on him, but he waited silently for him to begin.

"With Mikhail's untimely demise," Radoff said, "our arrangement has been compromised."

"I'm sorry about your son," Viktor offered.

Radoff waved away the condolences. "I'd like to see our families united still."

Viktor nodded. He expected this, knew Radoff's ambitions drove him to eschew Russian traditions. Still, even he must know offering Katria to Pavel was a bad omen. Not that Viktor was opposed to it, but he needed space and time before agreeing.

"There's no rush," he said confidently. "Let's wait until after Lent."

"I have no interest in waiting," Radoff said coolly. "Nor do I need to. There's nothing to be done to bring Mikhail back."

"What do you propose?"

"The same agreement as before: a union between Katria and my son." Viktor offered a confused look though he knew full well what Radoff offered. "My son Pavel," Radoff clarified.

Katria loathed Pavel, despised him in every way imaginable. And Viktor was not certain she would survive one year of marriage with the younger Radoff son. Pavel's reputation preceded him as the Russian winds preceded winter. There'd been more than one rumor of Pavel beating his lovers, and even beating one so severely she died from the wounds.

Then again, it didn't matter what happened to Katria once the alliance between families was established. Constantine, however, was a different beast altogether. His son terrified him. The boy had contacts in the military and at court whom Viktor both feared and envied. He fully believed his son would kill him if it meant protecting Katria.

"I'm concerned," Viktor said, Constantine's threat echoing in his mind. It drove him to be equally cautious and shrewd. "I'm concerned with the idea of Pavel and Katria united. To switch from one son to the next so rapidly—Mikhail has only been buried a couple of days—will turn many heads. Plus," he said, choosing his words carefully, "Pavel is not known for taking care of his women."

Again, Radoff waved away Viktor's words. "Those at court who may have been aware we intended to pair Mikhail and Katria could easily forget, or be convinced they were mistaken and it was always to be *Pavel* and Katria."

Viktor believed it, but didn't voice his agreement. Pacing the room, he watched Radoff await his answer. Allying with the Radoff name had its advantages, but given the recent turn of events, Viktor didn't wish to rush into another betrothal. Damn the girl! When his wife bore Katria, Viktor never envisioned it would be this difficult to marry her off.

No, he thought as he returned to the sideboard. He poured another glass of vodka but didn't drink it. No, he'd wait. Give her time to properly grieve the loss of her fiancé. Then he'd see what match would be most advantageous.

"I'm not opposed," Viktor eventually said. "But I don't wish the tsar to perceive this as anything other than what it is. Give the girl until after Lent," he repeated. "Then we'll talk."

****

Katria was safe.

Nikolai paced the study like a caged animal, restless, unable to do anything more for the moment. He needed to see her, but trusted Constantine to protect her until he could. Taking this opportunity to delve into Peter's death, he bided his time.

With Mikhail dead, and Markova not announcing yet another betrothal, Nikolai felt he finally had a little time to gather his forces. He fully intended to attack Viktor and marry Katria whether it was with his permission or not.

"Excellency," Lev, the butler, intoned in a shaky voice. Nikolai looked up at the man, who insisted he was well enough to continue his duties despite the beating Markova's ruffians had inflicted on him. "The servants have arrived with the carriage."

Nikolai nodded, not trusting himself to say anything. Lev looked pale, but he couldn't tell if the butler was still recovering from the beating or if the arrival of Peter's carriage sickened him.

"Have they restored it?" he managed.

"No, Excellency," Lev said. "I believe they waited on your instructions."

"Have them store it," Nikolai said. He didn't want to see it, didn't want to be reminded of Peter's death, the ignoble way he died.

"Wait." Lev stopped. "No," Nikolai said. "I need to see it. Have them pull it round to the alley."

Accepting the overcoat Lev held out from wherever he'd hidden it, Nikolai walked with heavy steps through the hall. Dread settled in him, and he wondered why he bothered. His steps echoed through the empty house. Walking down the street to the alleyway, Nikolai turned the corner to see the carriage.

How the footmen managed to move it—in one piece—from wherever the Third Section stored it in the Palace to here, he didn't know. The carriage itself wobbled on the metal suspension, the left side smashed in, making it unsteady. The hitch was broken in several places, and the horses neighed in the winter afternoon, the temperature made all the colder given the shadow of the alleyway.

Sorrow welled within him, and Nikolai swallowed against the emotion. He took a step toward the carriage, then stopped.

Running his hand over the cracked and scarred wood, he noticed the missing window glass. His family crest split along the line of the broken door. He peered into the interior, eyes immediately moving to the location of the light fixtures. The left one was missing, torn from its place. It had been tossed on the floor; blood still stained the gray base.

What had he hoped to accomplish by looking at the carriage? What had he thought to see in its mangled carcass and torn bits of finery?

Nothing.

His breathing sounded loud in his ears, and he imagined he could hear Peter laughing. That laugh turned into screams as the carriage tilted, turned over. Crashed into whatever it collided with.

Shaking his head, Nikolai stepped out of the alley and into the sunlight. Blinking against the sudden change, he nodded at the footmen. "Destroy it."

He had no need of it.

Turning, he walked back to the house, knowing full well the servants would take whatever was left of the heavy curtains and gold trim. He didn't care. They could take the whole damned thing if they wanted, so long as he never saw it again.

What in hell had Peter been doing in St. Petersburg weeks before he'd said he'd arrive? What papers did he carry? Nikolai cursed Lazarenko and Terenov—and himself. But in spite of the fact that Lazarenko could be bribed, he wouldn't show the papers to Nikolai. And where was Uncle Alexey?

Peter had worked for Alexey. Nikolai was certain of it.

Halting in the snow, he jerked around. Already he heard the creak of the carriage as his footmen dragged it out of the alley.

Peter wasn't a stupid man. If he had carried incriminating papers on him, he'd have hidden them in *case* of just such an accident. And if he carried papers that could implicate another, he'd also have hidden them.

Running back to the alley, Nikolai shouted, "Wait!"

Wrenching open the right side door, Nikolai scanned the interior. Climbing into the shaky carriage, he peered into the hole where the light fixture once hung. Nothing. Empty. Probing the top, he searched for anything amiss, anything that bulged or didn't feel as if it was supposed to be there.

Still nothing.

Growling, knowing he was right, Nikolai felt along the seats, between the back and the cushion. Nothing. Trying the opposite side, he was about to give up hope.

There.

Heart pounding, he said with a grin, "Peter, you sneaky bastard."

Yanking at the seat, he found the crumpled stash of papers. Shoving them into the inside pocket of his overcoat, he exited the carriage and nodded to the servants. Laughing, he strode back to the townhouse.

****

Katria walked into the Orlov townhouse, somewhat surprised Nikolai wasn't there. She didn't let her disappointment show as Constantine's carriage moved away and the butler took her cloak and gloves.

"He's in the study," Lev said, bowing and discreetly disappearing.

Nodding her thanks though the man had already turned his back, Katria walked down the hall. Nikolai was hunched over his desk, gaslight blazing next to him as he read a stack of papers. His coat and vest were draped over the chair and his shirt sleeves were rolled to the elbows. He didn't look up at her entrance. With a wicked grin, she moved as quietly as possible around the desk.

Leaning over him, she whispered, "Hello, lover."

His hand was on her wrist before the last syllable of *lover* left her mouth. Where the knife came from, Katria didn't know, but it was at her throat before she blinked. Surprised, she couldn't move, could only gape down at him.

Nikolai seemed to recognize her before she fully recovered and, looking sinful and delicious, pulled her onto his lap, mouth on hers. Unbalanced, Katria returned the kiss, shifting as best she could in her gown to pull him closer. His hands held her still, and she felt the smile against her lips.

This was their first time together since Mikhail died. Feeling his shoulders through his shirt, she trailed her hands down his back, up his broad chest. "I'm tired of being away from you."

"Good." She felt his light laughter along her skin as he kissed down the side of her neck. Pulling back, he looked serious. "I don't want you in Viktor's household no matter how many times Constantine assures me you are well. I have a plan to take you out of St. Petersburg and to the German States. I have friends there."

Offering a brilliant smile, she kissed him lightly. "I've always wanted to see Prussia, and I hear Saxe-Coburg and Gotha are lovely." Then on a more serious note she said, "The gossip of the court has moved on to the topic of the day."

"But it will return to us," he said. Turning her on his lap, he showed her the papers he had been looking through.

Spread out on the large desktop, she glanced at the first one, but it made no sense. Ledgers in neat little columns, conversions: rubles, Ottoman kurush. The next page she grabbed had a list of names and amounts next to each name. It took her a moment to understand what they meant.

"Are these the papers Peter carried?" Her voice was soft, awed.

"Yes." His lips traced the back of her neck, up to her ear.

"Where did you find them?"

"In the carriage," he said. Undeterred, he kissed along her shoulder line and Katria was suddenly grateful she wore a low-cut evening gown. Nikolai pulled away, and she bit back a moan of frustration. "They were hidden behind the seat. I'm convinced Peter was murdered."

Turning, Katria looked over her shoulder. "Murdered." She didn't ask, already knowing he was correct. He nodded slowly, but she saw a glint in his dark eyes she couldn't quite make out.

"They point to Radoff," he said.

Revenge. His eyes shone with revenge.

"You suspect Radoff of killing Peter?" she asked.

Nikolai nodded, one short movement of his head. "I'm convinced. But I want to play this carefully."

"Oh?" Katria asked. "*Ohh.*" With Radoff dead, there was no exoneration of Nikolai, of Peter. Her smile was slow, matching his wicked one. "How can I help?"

Chapter Ten

CONSTANTINE DIDN'T care that he was interrupting. There'd be time enough for Katria and Nikolai to be alone after they took care of this treason business. However, seeing her sitting on Nikolai's lap, his mouth on her shoulder, sparked a protective surge within him.

"I don't want to see this," he said.

With a final kiss to her neck, Nikolai set a furiously blushing Katria on her feet and stood beside her.

"Peter's carriage was returned today," Nikolai said.

The other man ignored Constantine's glare. Smug bastard. At least they were getting married—one way or another.

"When I searched it, I found the real papers he carried." Nikolai shook his head, gathering the papers scattered along his desk. "I knew my brother wasn't that stupid, wouldn't be caught off guard."

Taking the documents, Constantine skimmed through them. "Where?"

"Behind the seat." There was a buoyant tone to his voice that had been missing these last weeks. Constantine snorted in laughter.

"They point to Radoff."

Snapping his head up, Constantine looked at Nikolai. "Radoff? It makes sense, but Sergey is too intelligent to leave behind evidence. The mere fact Peter had these and managed to hide them from Sergey, or whomever Sergey sent, surprises me."

"Don't be surprised," Nikolai said. "Peter was more skilled at deception than most were aware."

"We suspect Radoff is behind Peter's *accident*," Katria added.

Constantine nodded, expecting this. He shuffled through a few more, scanning the lists of numbers, the pages of names with amounts printed neatly beside them. Bribes, no doubt. Correspondence between an unnamed man—Radoff—and several high-ranking Ottoman generals, including General Pasha and the French Marshall, François Certain Canrobert.

"Now we need to get this evidence into the right hands," Nikolai continued. He walked around the desk to lean against it, arms folded. "I can't very well go into the Third Section myself, and if either of you do it, it'll be suspect."

Handing the stack to Katria, Constantine absently wandered the room. He saw his sister place the papers on the desk, then stand beside Nikolai. She'd changed, too; he could see it as clearly as he could envision the military tactics he ordered. Though they didn't touch, it was clear they'd been intimate. The closeness between them wasn't forced or faked.

Hell, he thought, trying to figure out how to clear Nikolai's name with these new documents, *they didn't have to touch to show they loved each other*.

"I know several in the fourth department, the lower ranks in the Third Section," he said, thinking it through. "If they claim to find the papers, if they follow up on the carriage, it'll open a path to Lazarenko, then the tsar."

"Shame your uncle isn't in the city." Katria sighed. "This would have been cleared up days ago."

"But you're right," Nikolai nodded. He rounded the desk to the safe hidden behind the Pushkin first editions. "That seems to be the best course of action." Nikolai offered him a stack of rubles. Flipping through the papers, he kept several and handed the rest to him.

"Suspicion will be diverted to the Radoffs," Constantine said, grabbing the folio off the desk.

"Let the rumors devour them," Katria said with contempt.

Constantine agreed, but wanted to accomplish this as quickly as possible. Kissing Katria on the cheek, he bid Nikolai goodbye and left.

On the ride to the Palace, he read through the rest of the records Peter either stole or copied. No wonder Radoff wanted them back so desperately, the treasonous bastard. From what Constantine gathered, these were nearly identical to the ones found near Peter's body. Ledger amounts, letters. How had Radoff known which were stolen? Or had he forged the most obvious, the most incriminating?

Slipping them into the folio, he drew back the curtain and watched the Winter Palace. The columns passed by and he tried to guess what rooms hid behind the multi-layered façade. The night was clear and the moon reflected off the snow, illuminating the gilt. Courtiers came and went, none sending his carriage more than a passing glance.

They rounded the Palace to where the Third Section offices lay. A pair of guards stood beside the one door in the Palace with little obvious activity. Barely waiting for the horses to stop, Constantine leapt from the carriage and headed for the door.

He knew Petrovin worked the overnight shift; he was too far down the hierarchy to do otherwise. What he didn't know was whether his contact was in the offices tonight, or out spying for the tsar. Nodding to the guards, Constantine entered the first-floor offices. As was usual after nightfall, the rooms were nearly empty save for those few officers.

Smiling and nodding to several he knew, he spotted Terenov. Turning in the other direction, he continued his search for Petrovin. With a quick glance over his shoulder, Constantine walked to Petrovin's desk.

"I received correspondence from my first lieutenant," Constantine said, tucking the folio under his arm and casually leaning against the man's desk. "Seems your brother is seeing a local woman."

Petrovin looked up and laughed. "Doesn't surprise me," he said. "He always has a new woman."

He resisted looking over his shoulder to where he knew Terenov sat. "You busy tonight? I'm restless. Are the kitchens open? I'm in the mood for some apple babka."

"Of course," Petrovin said, stacking his transcribing and locking it in his top drawer. "My grandmother used to make bilberry babka." He sighed. "So delicious, you never tired of it."

They'd cleared the offices, wandering the labyrinth of hallways to the Winter Palace's kitchens. When he was certain they were as alone as possible in the Palace, and hadn't been followed, Constantine stopped the other man.

"I've something sensitive to discuss," he said in a low voice. "I just came from Nikolai Orlov's—we searched the carriage his brother died in and discovered a stash of papers. I assume Peter managed to hide them before the accident."

Petrovin nodded, interested. He stepped closer and asked in an equally low voice, "What papers? I've heard rumors, but even among the Third Section, it's all speculation."

Opening the folio, he handed Petrovin the papers. "They implicate Sergey Radoff. There are letters between him and the Ottoman and French armies, statements of finance." Petrovin's head snapped up. "It's clear he's working contrary to Russia's interest."

"You speak of treason. If what you say is true," Petrovin glanced at the top page. "Count Radoff will be executed."

"After reading these, it looks like he deserves to be. But if I submit them through the proper channels, their origin will be tainted. However," he said as Petrovin looked through and discovered the stack of rubles, "if you came to the house to ascertain the carriage was properly delivered, and were present for and active in Nikolai's search of the interior, then you could submit these documents."

"I wasn't a part of this investigation," Petrovin protested. "If what you say is true, I don't want to be involved with *treason* or in having Count Radoff killed."

"Petrovin, this is the best way to give this proof to the tsar," Constantine insisted. Tapping the thick stack of rubles, he added, "The best thing to do for Russia."

Reluctantly, Petrovin nodded. "All right."

"Excellent," Constantine concurred. "I'll return in the morning. The best thing for you to do is get in contact with your superior."

"Yes. I'll return now."

Relieved, Constantine said with a smile, "I think I'll continue to the kitchens. All this talk of your grandmother's bilberry babka made me more hungry."

Petrovin offered a weak smile, but Constantine knew the bribe would bolster his resolve. Whistling as he walked down the ornate hall, he could all but taste the babka.

****

Paul Terenov, a suspicious man by nature, found the perfect match when he began working for Section One, the supreme police department of the Third Section. Now, as he surreptitiously watched the exchange between Constantine Markova and Petrovin, the little weasel, he blessed his father. *The old man should be proud*, Terenov thought as he tried to creep closer. He'd raised his only son to be exactly like him.

He couldn't hear more than a half dozen words, but had distinctly heard Count Radoff's name. When Markova passed the leather folio to Petrovin, Terenov's blood ran cold.

Flattening himself along the shadowed doorway, Terenov waited as Markova continued to the belly of the Palace. Petrovin's footsteps walked toward another door, one that opened onto a courtyard. Thanking the tsar for not lighting the lower halls when not in use, Terenov followed.

Confident no one else lurked in the courtyard, he slipped up behind Petrovin. The other man read the pages by moonlight.

"What's this?" Terenov demanded, snatching the papers from Petrovin's startled fingers.

"I was at Court Orlov's," the other man stammered. "Making sure the, ah, property was returned safely."

"Property?" he demanded. "What are you speaking of, Petrovin? Make yourself clear."

"Peter Orlov's carriage was returned to his brother," Petrovin said in a stronger voice. "While there, I decided to do one last search of the carriage, sir. I found these pages wedged, ah, wedged behind a seat." He made a weak attempt to grab them back, but Terenov held them out of his reach.

"I was about to go to my superiors, sir," Petrovin added. Then, "Perhaps you can assist me, sir? There's quite volatile information contained within them."

Looking at the young officer, Terenov had a suspicion he wasn't going to like this. "What information?"

"Treason, sir."

"I see. We'll need to wake Lazarenko," he said, nodding.

"Yes, yes." The relief was clear in his voice. "I'll send for him immediately."

Closing the folio, Terenov stopped the eager Petrovin. "Just a moment."

Petrovin looked back. Seizing the back of his head, Terenov bashed it against the wall. A single moan escaped his lips, and Petrovin died quietly.

"You shouldn't have listened to Markova," he said, crouching beside the body. He pocketed the thick stack of rubles, raising his eyebrows at the bribe Markova offered in Orlov's defense. Sighing, he looked around the courtyard. "Now I'll have to dump you into the Neve."

****

Katria kissed Nikolai's chest. She stretched, luxuriating in the feel of him beside her, of his hands as they leisurely stroked her back. Never had she felt so relaxed, so...

"Hmm," she sighed and kissed his chest again. Her fingers trailed along his shoulders, down to his stomach.

"I hope it all goes smoothly," she said, looking up at him.

Nikolai's left eye opened and he peeked at her. The look, wickedly arousing, had her leaning over to nip his lower lip.

"This is the first time in weeks I feel as if everything's right," he said, rolling so she lay beneath him.

Frowning up at him, she shook her head. "So long as nothing unexpected happens." All her sated happiness vanished. "When's Constantine to return?"

Nikolai didn't move, but watched her for long moments, dark eyes unreadable. "Not too much longer," he promised.

She nodded, trusting him but worrying for her brother. But then Nikolai's mouth closed around her nipple, and his teeth tugged hard. Gasping his name, she arched off the bed. With a boldness she wouldn't have expected of herself before she met Nikolai, Katria pushed him off so he lay on his back.

Hovering over him, she bent to explore. Looking up at him through her lashes, she whispered, "My turn."

****

Sergey Radoff sat in his favorite chair, drinking a glass of French brandy, and reading Evgeny Baratynsky's *Eda*. While not as powerful as Pushkin, and so few were, Baratynsky was much less sentimental. Sergey believed it the cleaner read.

Pavel stood over the desk, looking at a map of their lands along the Dnepr River. He'd been obsessed with them since Mikhail's untimely demise. Poor Mikhail; who knew the man was prone to seizures?

"Here," Pavel pointed to the map. Sergey looked over at his son, but didn't rise. "This is the most fertile of the Markova lands. I'll build a new manor for Katria and me."

"Excellency," the butler interrupted.

Before Sergey bothered to stand, Terenov of the Third Section barged into the room. The butler huffed at the undignified intrusion, but Sergey waved him away. With a long-suffering sigh, he rose.

"Terenov?"

"Count Constantine Markova nearly succeeded in having you executed for treason." Terenov tossed a folio at him. It dropped to the floor with a thud. "These were discovered in Peter Orlov's carriage."

Composure threatening to crack, Sergey nodded to Pavel to pick them up. He needn't bother to look through them; he already knew what they contained. Damn Orlov! Damn the lot of them!

In an icy voice he demanded, "What happened?"

"Markova passed them to an officer he knew," Terenov said, "Petrovin."

"Has anyone else seen them?"

"Not at the Third Section," Terenov confirmed. "Markova recruited Petrovin, who's currently under the ice in the Neve River. Markova and Orlov—*Nikolai* Orlov—have seen the folio."

Cursing, Sergey tried to regain his self-possession. *Damn it!* Snatching the folio from Pavel, he tossed it into the fireplace.

"Take care of Constantine Markova tonight!" he ordered Terenov and Pavel. "We'll take care of Orlov later. No one will listen to him."

Terenov nodded and disappeared. Pavel returned to the sideboard and poured himself more vodka. "Can you trust Terenov to complete the job?" he asked.

"I trusted *you* to take all the papers in Orlov's carriage," Sergey snarled, snatching the glass out of Pavel's hand and throwing it against the wall. "Terenov is being paid handsomely. He'll do what he's told."

Pavel frowned, but didn't pour more to drink. "What of Nikolai? We should kill him, too."

"It's not time yet. Don't worry about Orlov. We don't want it to be too obvious."

Chapter Eleven

CONSTANTINE RESTED his head against the seat as the carriage pulled out of the Palace. It moved more slowly than usual, but then he was tired and wanted his bed. Since returning to St. Petersburg, he'd done nothing but move from military matters to personal or political matters. He'd forgotten how busy court life was, even compared with combat.

At least Katria and Nikolai had more time together. Ah, what he did for love and family. Still, it was late and he needed to pick up Katria and return her to Viktor's before their father decided to grow a spine and get her himself. The sleigh pulled through the snow, the movement lulling him into a light sleep.

He woke with a jolt when the carriage made a sharp left turn. Something wasn't right. Another left turn; they came too quickly. Shaking the sleep from his mind, Constantine peered out the window.

The snow-covered street didn't look familiar.

Peter died in a staged carriage accident.

At that thought, all sleep vanished. He pounded on the roof of the carriage with his walking stick. Damn it, what was Katria's driver's name?

"Driver!" he shouted. "Stop the carriage."

The man, if it was indeed Katria's driver, ignored him. Cursing himself for not bringing his pistol, Constantine drew his saber and opened the door.

"The river?" he muttered.

This wasn't going to end well.

The carriage jolted to a stop and Constantine jumped out. Holding the sword high, he approached the driver's box. It was vacant. Glancing quickly around the empty area, he started to climb into the seat. Not taking any chances, he was going to drive the carriage himself.

Sword in one hand, he heaved himself up. The bullet ripped through his left shoulder.

Falling backwards into the snow, Constantine struggled to sit up, to clear his mind. Pain exploded behind his eyes, fire licked along his arm, but he wasn't going to let the bastard who did this win. Maneuvering his sword to help him stand, he collapsed back to the ground as it was kicked out of his hand.

"Omph," he mumbled.

Grabbed from behind and lifted up, Constantine tried to turn, but his assailant punched him in his wounded shoulder.

"Son of a bitch," he managed, trying to remain conscious.

They were going to throw him into the river, he realized. But he couldn't stop the other man from dragging him along the bank and shoving him in. The water, so cold it felt like hot pokers against his exposed skin, enclosed him. Gasping for breath before going under, Constantine felt the current already dragging him down.

Clawing and scratching at the ice, he felt as if he lay in his own coffin. Pushing at the ice, he tried to punch through it. Though the water dragged at him, he refused to let it stop him. With only moments left, he tried to find a weakness, a crack, something. His lungs hurt and with as much force as he could manage, he punched up, surely breaking his hand.

The ice would not give way.

Regardless of the pain he felt, he continued searching. There. A crack. Using his injured hand, he punched along the weakened ice, and even with the extreme cold, pain reverberated through every inch of him. He relished the pain—he was still alive.

Again and again he hit the ice until it cracked open enough for him to squeeze through. Weak, exhausted, he pulled himself up. He lost his grip and slipped back through.

"Damn." The curse was weak, and he knew not much time remained. He was dying.

Wrenching his knee through the hole, Constantine hauled himself through, panting, and fell on the ice. He tried to call out, tried to move, but couldn't. If he stayed along the edge of the Neve much longer, it would swallow him again. And he knew he hadn't the strength to survive another trip beneath the ice.

He couldn't feel his entire left side, but Constantine dug his fingers into the snowy banks and crawled. He heard something above him, along the street.

"Help!" he screamed.

The noise didn't abate, and he tried again. Drained, he rested his head against the snow. "Help!" he called.

Scuffling, and voices, louder. If he attracted the attention of whoever tossed him into the river, he couldn't fight them off. He could only pray it was someone who would help him, rather than steal from him and leave him for dead.

****

February 17, 1855
Georgian Calendar

The clock struck one. Katria paced before the banked fire, twisting her hands in her wrinkled skirt. Nikolai watched her, but could offer no words of comfort. Constantine was late in retrieving her. Even if it took him longer to convince his contact of the validity of the documents, it was long past the time he'd promised to return.

"Something's happened," Katria said for the fifth time in as many minutes.

Nikolai knew, but didn't know what to tell her. Stopping her pacing, he held her by the shoulders.

"We should have done this hours ago," she said, but didn't break away. "Let's go to the Palace."

Nikolai nodded, and he could sense the frantic fear in her. He didn't think it was a good idea; Constantine might already be working with his contact and Lazarenko on arresting Radoff. He rang for the butler and called for the carriage. As they waited, she resumed her pacing.

"Maybe I should return home," she said. "See if they received word there."

Nikolai bit back the curse condemning Viktor for not sending a messenger if, indeed, he knew what had happened to Constantine. He also didn't correct her: *this* was her home now.

"I don't want you returning to that house alone," he snapped. Softening, as it wasn't her fault he worried for Constantine, he added, "We'll find Constantine first."

She stepped into him, resting her head against his chest. Surprised, Nikolai wrapped his arms around her.

"I won't let anything happen to you," he whispered.

"I know." Katria stepped back, new excitement on her face. "What if Constantine already had Radoff arrested? What if the Third Section is working with him? If we arrive there, we could ruin everything." She shook her head, paced again. "Maybe we should wait until morning when it'll be less suspicious."

Accepting her change of heart, Nikolai nodded. It was for the best, but if she wanted to storm the Palace to find her brother, he'd go with her. Ringing for the butler, he canceled the carriage.

"Come," he said to Katria, taking her hand. "You're staying here tonight."

"Why, Count Orlov." She grinned. He could see concern in her eyes for Constantine, but she accepted his hand and offered a wanton smile. "How scandalous."

****

Nikolai watched Katria. After they made love last night, she'd fallen into a fitful sleep and he was loath to disturb her. The discreet knock on his door alerted him the footman had returned.

Lev stood there, looking grave. "I'm afraid there's no word, Excellency."

"Where's the man?"

"Below."

Nikolai took the steps two at a time, bursting into the parlor and startling the footman. It was the same man who had followed Markova's peasant guards. "Well?"

"I'm sorry, Excellency. Count Markova is not at the offices of the Third Section, nor the military offices, nor the state rooms. As far as I've been able to tell, he's nowhere at the Palace."

"Damn it," Nikolai breathed. "Where the hell can he be?"

He feared his friend was dead. He trusted Constantine and knew he would never betray Katria. How the hell could Radoff have found out? Was he watching the house? Had one of his own servants betrayed him?

Nikolai eyed the footman, but the man gave away nothing.

Not me, he realized. *Constantine*. Someone in the Third Section, either Constantine's contact or someone the contact trusted, had betrayed Constantine.

"What have you found out?"

Katria's voice cut through Nikolai's thoughts. Now fully dressed, she entered the room. The footman bowed and backed out. She looked beautiful, dressed in the previous night's gown, hair long and wild down her back.

He went to her, but she backed away. "What have you discovered?" she repeated in a stronger voice.

Taking a deep breath, he said, "Constantine isn't at the Palace."

"Then where is he?" she demanded, her voice rising with panic. "He can't have just vanished!"

"I don't know," Nikolai admitted. "But I intend to find out. Stay here. I don't want you leaving."

"I have to go back," she said urgently as she gripped his hand. "I have to go home. If Constantine is there he might be injured. He might need me."

"I don't want anything to happen to you and I don't trust Viktor. Stay here. I'll check the Palace myself."

She caressed his cheek, and though he could see the worry in her eyes, her voice was soft. "There are four people I cherish in the world. Constantine is one of them. I have to do all I can to ensure he's all right."

Nikolai pressed a hard kiss to her mouth. "Stay here," he repeated. "I promise I'll do all I can. I'll find him."

****

Stalking down the Palace hallways, Nikolai felt useless. Constantine wasn't in the Third Section offices, he wasn't in the state rooms, and no one had seen him in days. Or claimed to have, at least. Heading for the military offices, Nikolai spotted Piotr Denlev.

"Denlev! Were you here last night?"

"Orlov?" Denlev shook his head. "Yes, I was here last night, and half the damned morning, too. That bastard Petrovin disappeared and nobody's seen him since."

Nikolai stepped forward, startling the other man. "Have you seen Count Markova?"

"Markova?" Denlev frowned. "Yes. I think he spoke with Petrovin, but then the damned man disappeared. Terenov may know. He went after them."

Nikolai stepped back. *Terenov.* He should have known. Nodding to the other man, Nikolai abandoned the military offices. He'd kill the bastard—after he discovered Constantine's whereabouts.

Terenov wasn't in the Palace; Nikolai would bet his life on it. Heading for his carriage, he instructed the driver to head back home. He needed Terenov's address, but didn't want the request connected to him.

The moment the sleigh pulled to a stop, he jumped out. Upon opening the door, he knew Katria had left. The house seemed emptier, and she didn't rush to meet him, didn't call out. Fury and fear battled within him. He knew he shouldn't have left her alone. Lev appeared and he rounded on the butler.

"Where is she?" he roared.

"She left, Excellency. I believe she went home."

****

Katria searched the house. Her father managed to hire more guards, she noticed with a private smile. He was afraid of Nikolai. Good.

She didn't speak with the servants, didn't ask them if they'd seen Constantine, but silently moved from room to room seeking him. He wasn't in the house. Viktor, however, sat at the breakfast table, newspaper open before him, a half empty plate of food beside him.

The room was empty except for him. Without a word, she turned to leave.

"It surprises me your brother would keep you out all night," her father said.

"We were separated during the night," Katria half lied. "Has he returned?"

Viktor raised an eyebrow and set aside his toast. "Out alone all night?"

Katria, unconcerned with what he thought, left. He didn't know anything about Constantine's whereabouts.

Her nerves were getting the best of her; she wasn't accustomed to worrying about those she cared for. What should she do? Return to the Palace or Nikolai's? Summoning a servant, she requested her cloak and had the man call a carriage.

She didn't want to stay there a moment longer. "I should have stayed at Nikolai's," she mumbled to herself. She paced the foyer, fingers twisting the folds of her gown. Where was the servant?

She felt as if she were being watched and whirled to see her father standing silently in the shadows.

"Constantine is dead."

The words hung between them. All breath left her body and her knees threatened to buckle. Katria refused to believe him, yet the confident tone of Viktor's voice…

"His carriage and sword were found by the river," he continued ruthlessly. "Blood spattered the area. Must have been a robbery."

With a cry of anguish, she launched herself at her father. "Did you do it?" she screamed, clawing his face. "Did you have someone hurt him?"

Composed even in the face of her grief and rage, Viktor captured her hands, smacking her across the face. She struggled to back away, but he didn't let go. Instead, he dragged her upstairs. Uncaring when she tripped on her skirts and fell to her knees, he pulled her up, slamming open the door to her bedroom. Tossing her in like an unwanted toy, he closed the door before she could get to her feet.

The locked clicked, and she was alone.

Chapter Twelve

NIKOLAI NODDED to his footman, whom he now knew was Lev's nephew. No wonder the man was so good at finding people. Lev had worked for his family for decades; Nikolai remembered his father saying that if he needed information, he had Lev uncover it.

Terenov's apartments were in a moderate part of the city, not too expensive for a member of the Third Section. Climbing to the second floor, he kicked in the door. Terenov was not in the front rooms. Ignoring the interior, Nikolai moved methodically through the rooms.

Papers lay scattered on an end table. Crossing to them, he quickly flipped through them. Unimportant. Just as he moved to toss them back on the table, Nikolai caught a glimpse of the bottom few pages. Forgeries. Not of the papers Peter carried, but of communication between an Ottoman general and...*Nikolai Orlov.*

Nikolai blinked and read them more carefully.

Troops moving to town Eupatoria, preparing for assault.

The rest were bits of news, some crossed out, some scribbled over top and along the side. It was obvious they were still in the process of forging the letter.

"Put the papers down, traitor." Nikolai looked up to see Terenov holding a gun aimed at his head. "You'll save me quite a bit of trouble, Count Orlov, if you'll just sign that."

Nikolai raised an eyebrow and shifted slightly. Terenov took a step forward, holding the gun steady.

"I had—"

Nikolai quickly raised his own gun and shot the bastard. Terenov fell to his knees, clutching his left shoulder. Kicking the gun from Terenov's hand, he picked it up and pressed it into the wound.

"Where's Constantine Markova?"

Terenov snarled at him, face ashen with pain. Nikolai smiled and dug deeper with the man's own gun. Terenov cried out, his eyes rolling back, but he didn't pass out.

"Where is he?"

Still nothing. After waiting several moments, until the other man recovered from his near faint, Nikolai shot him in the knee. Constantine was missing, and he dreaded discovering where his friend was. Katria was at her father's house and he didn't know what the old bastard would do to her. He didn't have time for this sniveling weak man. Nikolai had to protect what was his—had to protect Katria.

"If I tell you, you'll kill me," Terenov said through gritted teeth, sweat beading along his forehead, tears leaking from his eyes.

"Tell me," Nikolai offered, "and I'll spare your miserable carcass."

He took in a haggard breath and sneered, "He's dead. I killed him and tossed him under the ice."

Nikolai, fury blinding him, pressed the gun harder into the shoulder wound. He didn't believe him, didn't want to. He had to find Katria, get her out of the house, bring her home. Tell her.

"Radoff was behind this, yes?"

Terenov nodded, breathing worsening, and Nikolai knew the man was close to losing consciousness. Standing, he began to walk away. Terenov chuckled and said something Nikolai didn't catch.

Turning, Nikolai shot him in the head.

Constantine was dead. *Katria.* He had to get to Katria.

Nikolai gathered the papers from the side table. He wanted to burn them, but needed this proof. A noise grabbed his attention and he looked up, gun pointing at the doorway, to see Bishop Anatoli Mikhailivitch Markova standing there.

"What the hell do you know?" Nikolai demanded.

Anatoli closed the door, ignoring Terenov's body. "You really should close the door before interrogating…prisoners."

Nikolai growled, gun never wavering. Anatoli held up a hand, halting him, though Nikolai had little respect for a man of the cloth at the moment.

"I heard Constantine was at the Palace last evening. Then this morning rumors swirled that you had searched for him. It wasn't hard to track you here, Nikolai."

Completely disregarding the gun Nikolai aimed at him, Anatoli suddenly gripped Nikolai's overcoat. Slamming him back against the table, he demanded, "Where's my nephew?"

Nikolai dropped the gun. He didn't believe the other man knew about Constantine, or about the forged papers. Taking Anatoli by the shoulders, he told him. "According to Terenov, he's dead."

The bishop, strong, confident, and arrogant, wilted. His face whitened, his eyes narrowed. The moment of weakness passed and he exploded. "*Why?*"

"Radoff was behind all of it," Nikolai said. "Constantine was helping us—*me.*"

"I gathered as much." Anatoli nodded. He ran a hand over his face and shook his head as if to clear it. "Where's Katria?"

"She returned to Viktor's house to wait for Constantine." He retrieved his gun, picked up the papers, and admitted, "I hope she's returned to mine by now." Nikolai glanced back at Terenov's body. "Let's leave."

****

Katria was helpless. She didn't look it, but she most definitely was. Her hands weren't tied, she wasn't restrained to the chair, but she'd yet to move. Once, she shifted in her seat and the guard carrying the rather large knife took a step closer. She hadn't so much as coughed since then.

Pavel laughed as his father and Viktor Markova bartered.

"You're in a cage, my dear," he whispered to her, running his fingers down her cheek. Eyes the color of a stormy sea turned on him. "And we're the bars. I almost wished they had tied you to the chair."

Leaning closer, Pavel dragged his lips along her cheek, to her ear. "I know I plan on...*restraining* you every chance I get."

"We shouldn't delay the wedding until after Lent," Markova was saying. Pavel smirked at her, but she didn't flinch. "I'll dispatch a letter to the tsar as soon as I can, but I anticipate no problem."

"Excellent." Sergey nodded, toasting Markova with his glass. "We should be able to organize the wedding quickly. I'll arrange for the Palace chapel. Would the bishop be agreeable to performing the nuptials?"

Pavel watched Markova nod, but Katria made a sound. He turned to look at her, curious. Her face revealed nothing, eyes staring stonily ahead. Leaning toward her, he nipped her ear. Katria recoiled, fingers buried in the skirts of her gown. His laugh was low and soft.

"Hmm," he wondered aloud. "Did you expect help from that quarter? Did you think your uncle, the bishop, would help you?"

"I want grandchildren." Markova's voice came from beside him, and Pavel looked up.

"I have every intention of providing you one," he promised smoothly.

"Within the year. A healthy child," Markova added.

Unconcerned, Pavel agreed. "Within the year."

Satisfied, Markova returned to his father. Pavel returned his attention to Katria. "I plan on having you before the wedding," he whispered. His fingers drifted along the high neckline of her gown. He wasn't surprised she'd worn one that hid every inch of skin from his view. It was no matter—he could just as easily tear this off her as one with a more revealing bodice. "I plan to have you every night," he continued. "Every day. You'll be tied to my bed."

"If anything happens to Katria"—Markova's voice rose—"the child is mine."

"Agreed," Sergey said smoothly.

The child was his, but the land remained with the Radoffs.

"Excellency," the butler interrupted. "Bishop Anatoli Mikhailivitch Markova."

"Show him in," Sergey said. Pavel could hear the calculation in his father's voice, the joy at getting his way. "Show him in."

The bishop nodded to the room in general and waited while they all greeted him in the proper way. Pavel hated that, but if it meant keeping the smug bastard happy, he'd do it.

"I've come to speak with you and my dear niece," the bishop said, nodding gravely in Katria's direction. "I've heard there's been an incident."

"Before we discuss Constantine," Markova said, pouring his brother a glass of vodka, "the wedding between Pavel and Katria is set. We'd like you to perform the ceremony within the next week."

The bishop's eyes traveled to Katria, glazed over Pavel, lingered on Sergey, then came back to Markova. "Of course," he answered easily, accepting the drink.

Sergey nodded to him. "We should leave the family to their mourning."

Pavel nodded but whispered in Katria's ear, "It won't be long before I enjoy you."

****

"Bastards!"

Nikolai punched the wall, bits of plaster flaying off. He hit it again, not caring about the damage to his hand, his property. The study lay in shambles, just as his life lay around him. Peter was dead. Constantine was dead. Katria was lost to him.

He knew Viktor, knew the man wouldn't let her out of his sight until he married her off to the next available man. Tsar Nicholas wouldn't stop him, no matter how sympathetic he pretended to be toward Nikolai's plight.

Markova managed to hire additional men to guard his house. It'd take a small army to get her now. He'd planned just that, but Anatoli had advised him to wait, convincing him that something could be worked out.

Nikolai wouldn't have listened, save for the amount of respect he held for the bishop. But he couldn't rely only on Anatoli. Without Constantine as an ally, getting to Katria—

The wall cracked upwards as he continued to pound it.

Attacking Terenov, that peasant, and even Lazarenko was nothing. But to attack another member of the court, a minister at that, was unforgivable. He'd lose favor with the tsar forever and truly would have to leave Russia.

He would; in a heartbeat he would. But not without Katria.

"Excellency!"

Lev stood beside him, and Nikolai wondered how long it had been since his butler called him. Pain branched up his arms, along his heart. He couldn't stop beating the wall, and felt the pain of losing Katria when he did.

"Excellency," Lev repeated in a quieter tone and held out a glass and the decanter of brandy. Peter's best.

"I'm going to get her," Nikolai promised—himself, Lev, Katria. Taking the decanter, he poured a glass of his brother's best imported brandy and planned.

****

The Radoffs left, leaving behind the stench of their greed. Katria wanted to wash, needed to soak in a bath for the rest of the day to clean the feel of Pavel off her skin. She was going to burn this gown. If she could, she'd cut off the ear Pavel touched as well.

"I believe Constantine is dead, most likely tossed into the Neve, as many robbery victims have been over the decades," Viktor said to Anatoli. "I'll request a search, but hold no hope. And I'll not throw this household into mourning at this time."

He crossed to Katria and placed a consoling hand on her shoulder. Katria glared up at him but didn't move. "I don't wish my daughter to begin her married life under the heavy veil of mourning," he said. He patted her arm. "Come, child. There's much to do. And with your mother in the state she is, I'm afraid there's little time."

"Wait, brother," Anatoli said, holding up a hand to halt him. "I wish to speak with Katria alone."

She saw her father cast Anatoli a suspicious look, but he had no choice. "Very well. Don't keep her long. There's much to be done."

The moment her father left the room, keeping the doors open, Anatoli crossed and took her hand.

"You tremble, child." His voice was low as he tugged her, helping her to stand. "Come."

Drawing her to the windows, as far from the doors as possible, he said nothing. Incapable of halting her fear, she cracked. "Constantine."

"I'm sorry." With his back to the door, he effectively hid her from Viktor's view. "I don't want you to meet the same fate. I want you to protect yourself."

He pressed her hands again, and she felt a small vial. Quickly taking it, Katria slipped it into a hidden pocket. "Use it as you must."

Squeezing his hands in gratitude, she asked as quietly as possible, "And Nikolai?"

"He's fine, I promise you." Anatoli moved his hand to bless her. "We'll find a way to rectify this. Stand strong, child, and use everything I've taught you."

She kissed his cheek and watched him leave. The vial weighed nothing in her pocket, and she refused to touch it for fear Viktor would see. With a deep breath, she gathered her skirts and left the study for her rooms.

Passing Viktor in the hall, she glared at him but he ignored her. The guard assigned to her this afternoon lumbered behind her, his heavy breath a constant reminder she wasn't alone. Once locked in her bedroom, Katria took out the vial of poison. Scanning her vanity, she opened a container of powder and nestled it within.

"I'll do whatever I have to."

Chapter Thirteen

February 20, 1855
Georgian Calendar

ANATOLI GESTURED for Nikolai to enter. Disdaining the ritual greeting, he nodded instead. Saying nothing, Anatoli allowed him this one slip. The man looked worse than he'd anticipated. Though he held himself straight, with his shoulders back, there were deep circles beneath his bloodshot eyes and harsh lines bracketed his mouth. His eyes, nearly black, blazed with passion.

"You've heard of the battle at Eupatoria?" he asked. "It was a pathetic disaster. The tsar is in a fit."

"I imagine." Nikolai's voice was harsh, and Anatoli wondered how much he'd had to drink in the days since he'd last seen him.

"The papers we discovered at Terenov's must have been authentic. I surmise they transposed the names, but there had to be communication between Radoff and our enemies. The element of surprise the tsar anticipated never existed. The Turkish lay in wait for our troops."

"Agreed." Nikolai shook his head. "Radoff is responsible for countless deaths and the dishonor of our army. If the emperor discovers this, the entire family will be put to death." Nikolai narrowed his eyes at him. "Unless you don't plan on telling the tsar?"

Anatoli shook his head, but didn't answer. He hadn't decided what to do with this information. The entire battle was a fiasco, and from what he learned, the tsar himself had a heavy hand in planning it. Still, with the proof of treason behind its failure, not all blame could be laid at his emperor's feet. However, Nicholas I, the Tsar of all the Russias, continued to plunge their country into this useless war.

Nikolai sat in a chair, head tilted back, eyes steady on the bishop's. Anatoli wanted to know what he thought, but the man was nearly unreadable. He had planned something: how to get to Katria and exact revenge on Radoff, and even on Viktor.

"There's more," Anatoli added.

Nikolai waited, perfectly still. Anatoli wondered if he knew, but no. He'd only just discovered this himself.

"Constantine is alive."

"What?" Nikolai stood, took a step forward, stopped. Shaking his head, he demanded, "How?"

"I managed to track him down last night," Anatoli said. "I found those who pulled him from the side of the river."

"And now?"

"He's recovering with people who are loyal to me."

"What happened?" Nikolai shook his head, rubbed a hand over his face. "Alive…how?"

"He was shot, thrown into the waters, left for dead. It's a miracle he pulled himself out." Amazed at the will to survive, at the strength his nephew possessed, Anatoli shook his head. "I asked Katria's friend Anna to stay with him."

Nikolai shuddered, and Anatoli could see a visible weight lifted off his shoulders. Gripping his arm, Nikolai breathed, "Thank God."

"While I share in your thankfulness…" Anatoli said slowly. The joy he felt at learning Constantine was alive was tempered by Eupatoria and the rest of the news he'd yet to share. With a sigh, he looked around the room, hoping his manservant had removed everything valuable.

"Katria is betrothed to Pavel Radoff."

There was a long silence after this declaration. Nikolai's eyes turned the deepest black, his hands curled into tight fists. Rage such as Anatoli had never seen, and had certainly never felt, came off the younger man in waves.

But Nikolai didn't move; Anatoli wasn't certain he breathed. Himself sick at the thought of his beloved niece with a man as cruel and vicious as Pavel, he waited for the explosion.

"How depraved is Viktor?" Nikolai asked in a low, dangerous voice. "He still believes his son is dead, doesn't he?" It wasn't a question, but Anatoli nodded. "I need to remove her from that household before he kills her!"

Anatoli stared at Nikolai. "While I don't disagree, you must tread carefully. I can delay this marriage for a short time, but decisions must be made."

****

All three Palace state rooms brimmed with activity. The chatter was at a near fever pitch, Nikolai noticed as he pressed through the crowd. He was greeted with curt nods and the occasional grin as he passed by. Obviously some people ignored him, others offered their hand and spoke of the lost battle. He stopped and listened to a few comments, unwilling to lose complete favor in court.

It wasn't long before he spotted his prey. With a nod and, "We shall speak later," Nikolai left the conversation in which he found himself and headed through the rooms again. Stopping a few yards away from the tsar and his son, Tsesarevich Alexander, he turned and greeted, "Pavel."

Pavel Radoff all but dismissed the young woman he'd been speaking with to turn and give Nikolai his full attention. "If it isn't the brother of the traitor," he whispered.

"Careful, Radoff." Killing him in the Palace was not a good idea, he reminded himself. But he could probably explain away the action. "I have no qualms about tearing out your throat here and now."

"What a sight that would be, Nikolai," Pavel taunted, "One that you may dream of, but one you can never achieve."

"You would be dazzled at the violence I could inflict on you." Nikolai stepped closer to Radoff, using his height to his advantage.

"Possibly." Pavel stepped to the side, circling Nikolai, "But if you attempt to take my life, everyone here would know who was responsible. You would still lose, Orlov."

"If you touch, Katria, I won't care," Nikolai grabbed Pavel's arm, squeezed.

Discreetly wrenching his arm from Nikolai's grasp, Pavel bared his teeth. "She is to be mine. What I do with *my* wife is none of your concern. *My wife.*"

"Harm her"—Nikolai leaned into the man—"and I will be sure to make her a very young widow."

Nikolai had nearly lost his precious control, but he left Pavel, nursing his arm, in the center of the courtiers.

Pavel was right about one thing, at least. He couldn't kill him. Not yet, not now. He'd already had his footman, Lev's nephew, begin trailing him. It was only a matter of time.

****

That had gone well, Sergey Radoff thought. He'd chosen the perfect moment to distract the tsar from talk of the defeat in battle. He saw it in Nicholas's face. Another word about Eupatoria, and the tsar may have ordered the rooms set ablaze. Sergey interrupted to inquire about Viktor Markova's letter requesting permission for Katria to marry Pavel.

Distracted, angry and clearly frustrated with the day's events, the tsar seemed relieved to speak of something other than the war. Almost immediately, he issued his permission and instructed an attendant to see to it in writing.

Glancing over at Pavel, who was inexplicably holding his arm, Sergey wondered just how Constantine's death would affect the wedding. As it stood, Markova said his son was missing, not dead. Perhaps they would be able to push the wedding along expeditiously.

****

The snow shimmered in the afternoon sun. Katria stared out the window, thinking of the time she and Constantine hurled their bodies into fresh snow banks. Laughing and playing until their legs could no longer support them and returning to Mother, one of the few times she was well, drenched and chilled through. A happy youth, when Father was at the Palace every day and they never had to see him.

Katria turned away from the memories and went to sit at her vanity. It hurt too deeply to think of Constantine any longer. Not now, not today; she needed to fortify her strength. She needed to polish her *veneer*.

Her maid crossed the room to her after storing the gowns she'd rejected for the day. Katria wanted to look the picture of innocence, give the air of the proper Russian daughter. The maid tended to her hair, long ringlets pinned back in a cascade of raven tresses, and she smeared a pale pink color on her lips. A bare hint of rouge on her fair skin and the blue-green earbobs to punctuate the blue-green of her eyes, and she was ready.

Standing, she smoothed the dark blue silk of her flounced skirt and checked the tied ribbons of her chemisette. It was time.

Once she stepped outside of her room, the guard Viktor had placed in the hall blocked her egress. "I am going down to see my father. Excuse me," she said in an even, but unthreatening tone. The guard stepped to the side and allowed her to pass.

The study door was open, she noticed as she came down the steps. She took a deep breath and proceeded toward her father. He glanced up at her as she entered and she acknowledged him with a nod before crossing to the table where the crystal decanters were. Taking one, she poured a glass of vodka, picked it up and placed it in front of her father. Moving to stand in front of his desk, a ritual she'd performed a thousand times before, she offered her most demure smile.

"Katria," Viktor started as he took the glass and downed the clear liquid. "I'm glad to see you have calmed. I'm convinced it was Orlov's influence that had you rebelling against your family."

"Yes, Father," she replied.

"I regret allowing Anatoli to convince me that engagement would be best. I hadn't had enough time to assess Nikolai Orlov. I knew his brother. We all did. Peter was a fine man, but Nikolai, he was a mystery. This is for the best. I will see to it that Pavel treats you well."

Viktor hadn't looked her in the eye again as he spoke of Nikolai and Pavel. He simply studied the account book opened on his desk. Katria waited perfectly still, eyes cast downward. Seething.

"We shall make arrangements for a service honoring Constantine after your wedding. I regret that it came to this. My son murdered by a random thief. It seems unfitting. But Constantine chose his side when he dared threaten my decisions. I will proclaim him dead in a few weeks, after you are married," Viktor continued.

Katria was amazed. Viktor was incapable of true remorse. He displayed a cavalier attitude toward his own son's death and maddening logic. Not to mention his disinterest in her marriage to Pavel Radoff and what she had no doubt he'd do to her.

"My hope is that you are swiftly with child. After you were born, your mother was unable to produce more children. And while she lives,

I am unable to take another wife." He let out a long-suffering sigh. "My position at the Palace keeps me sufficiently occupied that it has not been a problem until now."

She refilled his glass of vodka and retook her place in front of his desk. In the past, she'd learned a lot from his talking. He often thought her too slow to grasp all he said. She'd never paid attention to his crassness before, but now it brought home all the pain of the past.

"I've missed this. You were always such a pleasure to talk to before Orlov came into our lives."

With a delicate touch, Katria placed a small green vial on her father's desk in his full view.

"What is this, Katria?"

"Poison," she responded.

Chapter Fourteen

VIKTOR'S EYES snapped to the glass of vodka. His gaze switched to her, eyes widening as realization dawned. He sputtered for a heartbeat, a sight Katria never expected to see. She reveled in it for as long as it lasted. In the silence, a carriage rolled by and she heard a child shout.

"What did you do?"

"Father," she said calmly, a small smile playing around the corners of her mouth, "you are in no position to take such a tone with me." Retrieving the vial, Katria kicked the hem of skirt and moved away from the desk. Maintaining eye contact with the stricken man, she slowly circled the room. She did enjoy this supremacy she held over him—it offered her a measure of power and control over her own life.

"Such a simple matter to place a few drops in your drink."

"I am your father!" Viktor's voice was unsteady, panicked even. Her smile widened.

"In this family, we must all use whatever method we can to advance our position." Katria tilted her head toward her father. He should recognize the sentiment, if not the exact words. He'd spouted them often enough to her.

"You taught me that," she continued. "You taught Constantine as well. Constantine, by matter of his gender, was stronger than I." She paused before his desk and leaned over. "I needed to find a different method."

"Why do my children turn on me so viciously?" He hadn't released the glass, but held it with white knuckles. His face was an odd combination of white and scarlet. Katria wondered if he'd die from apoplexy and save her the trouble of threatening him.

"At any time," she continued, "I can put this in your drink or your meal. At the Palace. Anywhere a drop of poison can await you." She nonchalantly put the vial in her jacket pocket. "Remember how I cultivated my relations with the servants? Here, the Palace, so many places…one never knows, does one?"

Confusion danced in his eyes. Oh, this was priceless! Katria almost laughed, but this was too important.

"There are many who are loyal to *me*. And will do my bidding, Father. Without you being aware of it, I've caged you."

Pavel's words returned to her: *you're in a cage, my dear, and we're the bars*. The memory sickened her.

"If you dare move against me, you won't be alive to know you've failed. This is your single warning." She straightened, ensured she had his full attention and said, "Do not test me."

Viktor continued to sit there, fingers clutching the glass, angry, embarrassed, and—did she read that correctly? Impressed? He should be; all this was his doing. He'd taught her extremely well in matters of self-preservation.

"Dismiss the peasants you call guards. I shall be out all afternoon." She held her skirt and turned for the door. Over her shoulder she called, "Don't await my return."

****

The carriage turned the last corner to Nikolai's townhouse. Usually, Katria enjoyed the view along St. Petersburg's streets, the beauty of it, the diversity of the people. Today, the view passed by in a blur.

Constantine's death surrounded her, but she had little time to mourn. She would grieve, but it was a private pain and she refused to show her enemies how her brother's death affected her. She also refused to show her father.

What would she do now? Break her engagement with Pavel? Or take another route? Viktor was under her control and she could have exactly what she wanted. Nikolai. She desired him more than anything else in her life and she'd find an way to have him

The carriage halted before his townhouse, and anticipation quickened her blood. Handing her cloak to the butler, she went to find him.

Nikolai sat behind his desk, cleaning his guns. A thrill of desire rushed through her, though it had only been a short time since she'd last been in this house, and last seen him. Felt him. Now it felt like months.

Readying his guns wasn't how she expected to find him, but given all that had happened the last few weeks, Katria couldn't blame him.

"Nikolai."

He smiled slowly up at her, a wicked grin that melted her insides. "Preparing for war?"

He rounded the desk and held her tightly before she could blink. His mouth was hot on hers, his fingers soft against her face. She felt his restrained passion and his fear. Winding her arms around his shoulders, she kissed him back with everything she felt.

"How did you get away?" he whispered against her neck.

Her head fell back and she surrendered to the longing she had for him, the unending need. Was this how it always would be? Yes.

"I have my own tactics in war," she managed.

"I wouldn't have left you there," he said. Pulling back to look at her, she could see his seriousness. It was deadly. "I'd have gotten you by tonight."

Nodding to the guns on his desk, she smiled softly, knowing what he said was true. "I see that. Don't worry," she said, squeezing his hands. "I have Father under control."

He believed her, she could see that, but there was an underlying emotion in his dark eyes that confused her. Anger, a lethal promise to remove her from Viktor's house, but more. She was about to continue with their conversation, but suddenly realized…

Love.

The emotion was love. Panicked, she stepped back, but stopped before she did no more than shift her weight away from him. *Love.* It didn't panic her. That hadn't been panic; well, no more than a moment's automatic reaction. Nikolai loved her. She accepted it. Wanted it. Craved that love.

"Oh," she breathed.

Love. What they had done to survive together had been the definition of it, and only now did she appreciate it.

"What's wrong?" he wanted to know.

"Wrong? Nothing." Katria shook her head. No, there was nothing wrong. "Nothing," she repeated, with a smile on her face that widened.

"I spoke with Anatoli," he said. Only half listening, Katria nodded. "Constantine is alive."

"What?" She couldn't have heard him correctly. No, this whole love business had her imagining things.

Nikolai smiled but surely he wouldn't jest about something like that. Nodding, he took her chin into his hand, angling her so their eyes met. "I don't know who found him. Anatoli didn't say, but he was rescued from the banks of the Neva, shot, half drowned, nearly frozen to death."

"Where is he?" Katria broke out of his embrace, tugging his hand and heading for the door. "I have to see him."

"I don't know where, but he's with people loyal to Anatoli. Your friend, Countess Tiomkin, is with him."

"Anna?" Katria repeated, stumbling to a stop. Why had Anatoli asked Anna to watch Constantine? Why hadn't he told her instead?

No matter. None of that mattered. Shaking her head, she tried to maintain her composure. There was much to do. Constantine…

"Katria." Nikolai's hands were gentle on her face as he cupped her cheeks, his thumbs soothing as they swept under her eyes. "I'll take you to see him, I promise. As soon as it's safe." He leaned down and kissed her. "Please don't cry."

She hadn't realized she was crying. The shock of his words, the recognition of his love overcame her, and she released all the pent-up emotion. His strong arms enveloped her, holding her close. She felt his lips brush just below her ear, his breath hot against her skin, as he held her without saying anything. It was exactly what she needed, no meaningless words of sympathy or understanding.

He just held her.

Katria pulled back, looked up at him. Her skin quivered for his touch, her body yearned for his. Wiping the tears off her face, she stood on tiptoes and kissed him. His mouth was soft, probing, and she tilted her head, opening for his kiss.

Sensation streaked through her. Before she knew it, the top of her bodice was unbuttoned and Nikolai's hands covered her breasts, pinching the already hardened nipples into aching peaks that cried out for more. Teasing, tormenting, arousing, he walked her backward, laying her on the floor before the fireplace. His fingers twined with hers, but all Katria knew was his delicious mouth on her, the addictive taste of him, the need rising within her.

Her eyes drifted closed, her head fell backwards. Nikolai's short, blunt nails scraped over her nipples, teasing the soft underside of her breasts.

"Nikolai," Katria moaned, hips arching, striving closer to release.

Not enough. It wasn't nearly enough. His hands skimmed back up her body, tracing the bones of her jaw and cheek. More cool kisses, almost phantom in their feel yet indescribably real, covered her collarbone, her shoulder, down her arm to her inner elbow. Oh, yes, right there. She wanted to speak but could only gasp. Feel.

His mouth closed over one nipple, biting it before soothing it again and switching to the other. He teased her breasts, building her higher along the peak she craved and knew only with him.

His hand tangled in her hair, pulling her head even further back and exposing the long column of her neck. With a reverence that brought her closer to the edge, Nikolai placed cool whispered kisses there. She felt the mass of her skirts shift and bunch up, felt his large hand smooth down her side to tease her again.

"Beautiful," Nikolai whispered against her mouth.

When he left her lips, Katria cried out in frustration. But then he kissed her in that most sensitive of places, and she forgot everything.

"Please…Nikolai, please." She arched against him. More. She needed more; she was so close.

Slipping a finger into her wetness, he closed his mouth over her breast. Katria screamed as pleasure rocked through her. They joined in one smooth thrust.

Nothing in her life prepared her for the emotions she experienced when with Nikolai. Nothing had ever or could ever compare to this ecstasy.

They moved faster now, in one smooth rhythm. Katria felt herself flying, falling, and soaring into one heady tide after another. Crying out, she squeezed her innermost walls as her orgasm continued to wash through her.

"Nikolai," she cried in a whispered litany. Her hands touched his face as they shuddered together in completion.

Exhausted and sated, Katria floated. Nikolai slowly moved to one side and pulled her close. He held her, wordlessly, for a long while.

Katria rested her head against Nikolai's shoulder. The fire blazed hot against her back, her skirt bunched in uncomfortable places, but she couldn't move. Perfectly content to stay where she was for the rest of the day, she closed her eyes and let herself drift.

"There's more I need to tell you." Nikolai's voice woke her.

"Yes?" she asked, unable to raise her head to look at him. She really didn't wish to move.

"Terenov of the Third Section is responsible. When I searched for Constantine, I followed a lead to Terenov. I paid him a visit," he continued, and she could tell from the way he said *visit* it wasn't a pleasant meeting. "He worked for Radoff."

Her head raised, and she watched him through narrowed eyes. "Radoff." She should have known, should have guessed that horrible family was responsible for Constantine's death—attempted death. "And Terenov?"

"I took care of him."

"Good." She nodded once and laid her head back on his chest, uncaring what happened to the man who tried to kill her brother. "Everything leads back to Radoff," she mused aloud.

His hands tangled in her hair, bringing her up to face his again. "I won't let anything happen to you."

His voice was fierce, intense, and warmed her through.

"I know," she whispered, fully believing it. Kissing him, she reiterated, "*I know.*"

****

Sergey patted his horse's neck, speaking soothingly to the cold animal. This wasn't a part of town to show off as fine an animal as he rode, but there was no choice. Loose ends needed tying.

"I'll have the stable boy take extra care of you," he promised the horse, who snorted in agreement.

A sound behind him alerted him to another. "Have you done as I instructed?" Sergey demanded the moment his hired underling slipped around the corner.

"Yes, Excellency." The man nodded. "I burned all the papers you gave me to pass to Terenov. The man's dead."

"Yes," Sergey nodded in perceived sadness. "It's unfortunate. Are you certain there's nothing left with my name on it?"

"I swear it to you," the man continued and Sergey believed him. "There's nothing left. Everything's destroyed."

"Excellent." Sergey nodded. "Excellent. You've done well. Be sure to stay close should I need you again."

Handing over a small stack of rubles, he gave it to the man. Gratefully accepting it, the man flipped through the stack. Sergey, with a twinge of regret at disposing so smart a contact, pulled out his knife. In one swift strike, he stabbed the man in the neck.

Wrinkling his nose at the spurt of blood, Sergey stepped to the side, leading his horse so the beast wouldn't be fouled by the blood. Behind him, the man thumped to the ground. Looking over his shoulder, Sergey saw the blood stain the snow and knew he was dead.

Chapter Fifteen

KATRIA LEANED back into Nikolai's embrace. His fingers trailed over the bones of the corset he'd just retied. Hot breath caressed her neck as he held her. She knew he didn't want to let her go, release her to face the reality of their situation. With eyes closed, she indulged in the moment, indulged in the raw emotion between them, in the feel of his strength enveloping her.

"I've made all the arrangements and preparations," he said against the side of her neck.

Curious, she turned in his arms. "What arrangements?"

"To leave Russia." Nikolai brushed a strand of hair behind her ear. Katria rested her head against his hand. Leave? Then she remembered the plans they had made earlier. Prussia, Saxony, Saxe-Coburg and Gotha.

"The war complicates matters," he continued in a steady voice. "We'll need to take a train instead of departing via steamer. There shouldn't be any problems crossing into Poland as long as the tsar doesn't become involved before we leave Russia. From there, we'll head to Prussia or Austria, or anywhere else you wish to go."

"Constantine," she whispered. "I can't leave without seeing him."

"We will see him first, I promise. Anatoli will take us there." He moved his hand from her cheek and Katria felt the absurd notion that he left her, even though he walked only to his desk. "I've transferred funds out of the country and had Peter's estate settled."

Constantine—no, she couldn't leave her brother. Not when he need-ed her. On the other hand, to be with Nikolai, to marry him; it was too tempting to resist. But she couldn't. She couldn't do that. Not to her-self, especially not to Nikolai. Leaving would utterly destroy him—his name, his family. They'd never be able to return to Russia. They would never have a true home.

"You have made quite a number of plans, haven't you, Nikolai?" It wasn't a question. Katria approached his desk as she adjusted the sleeves of her chemisette. Oh, yes, she wanted to leave. But they'd both be destroyed if they did. "Plans that include leaving behind all you know."

"I have spent most of my life abroad, Katria. I will not regret leav-ing Russia." Nikolai opened a drawer to retrieve a stack of documents and slim books. His voice was firm, even. Not a speck of emotion col-ored his words.

Tilting her head, she fancied she knew him better than that. Nikolai was a master of hiding his emotions, but this wasn't like him; this was more than merely concealing his thoughts and feelings for the sake of court. This was between the two of them.

"This decision affects more than just our lives," she pointed out in a reasonable tone. "The rumors about Peter and your family have died down at court, true, but our leaving Russia will set fire to them."

She watched as he proceeded to prepare his documents. He listened to her, Katria knew, but it was as if he didn't care. Trying again, she said, "You'll leave Sergey Radoff, and who knows who else, with free rein to slander you and your family."

"That cannot be helped." His movements were methodical as he continued to scan the papers, stack them into two piles, and double check what looked like figures arranged in long, straight columns.

"And what of your Uncle Alexey?" she asked. Nikolai's fingers stilled, but only for a moment. "At some point, he'll return to St. Petersburg and return to heading the Third Section. You'll leave him exposed to ruin. The tsar may hold our betrayals over him."

Her voice held a tinge of sorrow, completely unfeigned. She knew Alexey only remotely, but he was a skilled diplomat and a close ally of Anatoli. And she knew Nikolai was close to him. So why did he insist they leave?

"We have not betrayed a *soul*. They have all betrayed *us*." He spoke the words in a hiss, anger obviously rising. Placing the papers on the desktop, he leaned on his hands and continued, "Alexey is a capable diplomat. He'll manage on his own."

"Why should he have to?" Her response was impassioned and she slammed a hand on his desk. Nikolai didn't flinch, and she saw more than anger in his eyes. "There is no fault here that lies with us! This is all the Radoffs' doing." Katria stepped away from Nikolai's desk and turned from him to take a deep breath. "Peter was my friend, Anatoli's friend, your brother. All he did was uncover their treason and they took his life for it! They attempted to frame him for their own crimes."

"Don't you think I know that?" he shouted. "Don't you think I know they were behind this? That they killed Peter?" He rounded the desk, took her by the upper arms and shook her. Emotion poured off him, the Nikolai she'd come to know. To want. To need.

"Don't you think I know all that?" he repeated. "Of course I do! I know they were also behind the attack on your brother, that because of *me*, Constantine nearly died, and may still!"

The blood drained from her face and Katria gripped his wrists. Somehow, she'd missed that, somehow she hadn't realized Sergey and Pavel were behind the attack on Constantine. Nikolai shook her again, and she wanted to demand he stop, but the look behind the anger stilled her.

Love. It was the love she saw before, still there, still strong. He'd yet to utter the words, had yet to tell her he loved her. But he did love her;

Katria could see it in his eyes. She recognized it in his actions and knew why he had done all this. It moved beyond their initial games.

"There's very little evidence left against them, Katria." He rested his forehead against hers, voice softer. "A single sheet. That's all I kept from the papers I found in Peter's carriage. What Constantine had has been lost. Destroyed, most likely. Terenov is dead, and the documents I found at his apartment are forgeries with my name on them. *Mine.* There are no witnesses, no further documents. We cannot legally move against them."

"I do not want to leave, Nikolai." She stared at him. "All of this... this *chaos* has been wrought by them. Peter's death, Constantine's near-death, the loss of favor, even the delicate balance I had achieved between Father and me over the years. All of it is their doing."

"I know," he said firmly. Backing up a step, he looked over her shoulder before returning to his desk. "I've considered staying to fight them. I'm willing to risk almost anything. However, there is one thing I am unwilling to risk."

He stopped and she knew. Before he said it, she knew.

"I won't risk you."

Warmth washed over her, and she took a step toward him, wanting to say something, wanting to respond. One thing stopped her; she refused to allow herself to indulge her feelings because he was wrong. Katria wouldn't let him destroy himself, his family, or the Orlov name.

She wouldn't let him do this for her. Wanting to rage at him, to call him a fool, she paused and thought it through carefully.

"That is not for you to choose." Her voice was hard, harder than she'd expected it to be.

Though she knew about and marveled at what he had risked, she hated that he had decided for the both of them. Hated that after all she'd done, all she'd managed in the preceding years, and in their own short time together, he still underestimated her.

"What risks I take are my own."

"They are not!" He came around his desk again, took her into his arms. "I love you! I love you and I'll not risk you!"

His fingers tightened on her upper arms, but his admission took her so off balance, Katria could only stare at him open-mouthed. Somehow, knowing he loved her was nothing compared with hearing him admit it.

"Not for revenge," Nikolai was saying now, "not for my name, not even for Peter's memory. Nothing else matters to me. *Nothing*."

"It matters to me." Her body shook from the emotion exploding between them. She was torn between wanting to hold him close, to make love to him again, to revel in the feeling between them, and wanting to slap him for using her in such a way. Katria tried words.

Framing his face with her hands, she stilled him.

"I now have control over Father," she said fiercely, shaking his head once. "This puts us in a far different position than we were in a short time ago."

"I don't care!" He held her arms, his eyes boring into hers. "I only care about you."

Her heart melted at his declaration, but she couldn't let him run. And she couldn't run. "Partner with me, Nikolai. Do not try to dominate me."

****

In need of a moment alone, Katria left Nikolai in his study and roamed the rooms of the townhouse. She could see the touches of a woman here, his mother no doubt, or perhaps a lover of Peter's she had no knowledge of; Peter had been a very private person. The wallpaper was new and the chairs were Gothic-inspired Chippendale, rather than the heavy Baroque of the furniture in the study and formal library.

As she wandered to the conservatory, her mind raced with thoughts of Sergey and all he'd done. The anger she felt threatened to consume her whole.

The scuffle of feet drew her attention and she looked up to catch a glimpse of one of the servants hurrying down the back stairs. She'd no time to consider what the servants might think of all that happened in this house of late. But then, she supposed they were as loyal to the Orlovs as her own servants were to her.

Stopping in front of a closed door, she pushed aside irrelevant thoughts about servants and opened it. What must have once been the morning room now looked abandoned. Again, there was a feminine touch to the room, although white sheets covered much of the furniture and the drapes blocked the sunlight from streaming in.

The wallpaper here was older, at least two decades out of fashion. She moved into the room, breathing in the stale air, letting her eyes adjust to the dimness. This room must have been used by Nikolai's mother.

Closed and cloaked in darkness, she considered the space. Abandoned. Shuttered. Without thinking, Nikolai had declared his love. Was she too angry to reciprocate? Was *she* too emotionally distant? Did she need his declaration so desperately so she could hold it close to her, warm herself with his words, and yet not return them?

"Katria!" Nikolai called.

Emerging from the morning room, she walked down the hall to see Nikolai standing with Anatoli in the foyer. How long had she wandered the rooms, lost in thought? How long had she wondered whether she could return Nikolai's feelings? Or whether she was as closed off as the morning room?

"Uncle." She took his hands and kissed his cheeks. "Thank you."

Looking around at the empty foyer, Anatoli nodded. "What are your plans?"

Nikolai ushered them into his study and closed the door behind them. She couldn't read him again, couldn't tell what he thought. He'd calmed; the anger and fear coming off him earlier were firmly shut behind his impeccable wall. Even the love. No, she realized as his gaze met hers. Not the love.

Never that.

"We'd like to discuss them with you."

****

"We need to rid ourselves of Nikolai Orlov." Pavel Radoff sat back on the sofa in the darkened room, the only illumination coming from the fireplace.

He preferred the dark, enjoyed drinking in it. For his more amorous activities, he lit the entire room, wanting to see his work. To be sure, darkness amplified the cries—both of passion and of pain. But the light, to see what he'd wrought, was worth the diminished sounds.

"Are you lying in wait for me, son?" Sergey pushed opened both doors leading into the parlor. He called for a servant to come light the candles in the room. Pavel scowled, but didn't contradict his father.

"Pavel," he said in an annoyingly reasonable voice, "moving against our enemy in such a bold manner is not advisable at this moment." Removing his jacket, Sergey tossed it on one of the brocade chairs, an elegant movement that showed his disdain for the clothing as much as for his only remaining son's words. "Your engagement has put you at odds with him, and the entire court is aware of that."

"That lot of the deaf and dumb will never suspect an accident or dare to question me." Swallowing the last of his drink, Pavel tossed his glass at the servant, enjoying his flinch as he lit the lamps on a side table. "That's enough light," he ordered. "Get out."

Picking up the glass, the servant turned to Sergey, who nodded and gestured for him to leave the room. Sneering at his father, Pavel stood. Wanting to contradict him, wanting the servants to obey him and not look to Sergey for permission, he remained impotent.

"Do not underestimate the deaf and dumb, as you call them. They can destroy you if you leave them an opening." Sergey's eyes narrowed, and Pavel knew the old man knew he was drunk. So be it.

"You're too cautious at times, Father." Pavel snapped, striding for the liquor tray and pleased that he moved in a straight line. "Tsar Nicholas is distracted by the war. Every one of them at the Palace is at odds with someone over something. Complaints about the generals, the shortages due to the blockade, the lost honor at Eupatoria." He knocked back his glass of vodka and poured another. "Orlov's death would hardly be noticed, much less investigated."

"This is not the time, Pavel. I have made my decision. Abide by it." Sergey turned and left the room. He ignored his discarded coat, as he did his son.

Weak though he was, maybe Mikhail had it right when he left. Still, as the only male heir to Sergey, if his father died…

"No," Pavel muttered into the now empty room. "Orlov is an annoyance." He rubbed his left arm, the one Orlov yanked, as he set down his full glass. "It's time I assert myself without consulting you, Father."

Chapter Sixteen

February 25, 1855
Georgian Calendar

SHE SCANNED the room. It seemed to Katria that she constantly looked through the Winter Palace's rooms for Nikolai and yet he rarely stood with her. This was her idea, she reminded herself. This was what she wanted.

Allowing herself to indulge in a fantasy of what it would be like to leave Russia with Nikolai, she could see them already in transit. Yes, by now they would be crossing the Russian Kingdom of Poland on their way to the Prussian lands and Kraków. On their way to anonymity. Where they could marry in peace, without seeking anyone else's permission or decree. It was a lovely fantasy.

Today, the crowd was especially thick. Ulensky invited everyone to her daughter's wedding. Including Nikolai, though Katria was certain she regretted that now. Alas, with so many in attendance, with the gorgeous view from the Great Hall onto the Neva, the old bat probably didn't care. Her daughter was married in the Winter Palace, and there was little else anyone of Ulensky's status and ambition could desire.

Allowing her gaze to travel across the smooth walls and columns, Katria wondered where her lover was. Through the throng of near-ly four thousand who drank expensive wines and Champagnes and awaited the sit-down dinner, she couldn't see across the enfilade into the other rooms, and moved closer to the bank of windows. Outside, the River Neva was a frozen ribbon. Once she had considered it beauti-ful, but now she could only think of Constantine in its icy depths.

"It won't be long before we're wed," Pavel said from beside her. Katria wanted to vomit. He'd followed her across the Hall even as she tried her best to avoid him. "I look forward to all we can do that evening."

"Your taunts are tiresome," she sighed, abandoning her search. "What do you hope to accomplish by continuing these sordid insinuations?"

"To unnerve you," he smirked. "I take great pleasure in preying upon the helpless rabbit in the meadow."

"What would you do," she asked, looking at him curiously, "if your prey *weren't* a helpless rabbit running away, but a wolf turning to fight?" She resumed scanning the room, though she needed all her wits to keep Pavel away. He had a disgusting habit of touching her.

"You do excite me, Katria," he whispered, stepping closer.

With a sniff of disgust, she stepped toward a hovering footman be-fore Pavel could touch her. Again. Mayhap it was just as well Nikolai wasn't in the vicinity. He'd have killed Pavel before their plan could progress. Katria sorely wanted him to kill her sniveling fiancé, but not until afterwards.

"And you do disgust me, Pavel." Gesturing for the scarlet-liveried footman to remain by her, she nodded to Pavel. "Take him to the tsar," she commanded. "Princess Ulensky monopolizes his time."

He snorted, still lingering near her. The look in his eyes told her that if he could get away with it in the Palace, he'd corner her and have his way with her. "I'm not a peasant," he scoffed and took a step closer.

Glad she hadn't anything to eat, Katria asked, "Have you not learned anything from your father?"

His eyes narrowed and she wondered what he *had* learned. She really did need to choose her words more carefully around the Radoffs, as they were apt to use every syllable against her.

"Use every opportunity to ingratiate yourself with our tsar."

Looking as if he wanted to protest, Pavel grabbed a glass off the footman's tray, spilling a few drops of liquid on her gloved hand, and stalked over to the tsar. Following him at a more sedate pace, she pasted on the most serene, regal smile she could manage. The footman followed.

Nicholas stood with Ulensky, nodding absently to the woman as she droned on about the wedding, the food, the graciousness of the tsar. Barely resisting rolling her eyes, Katria curtsied low before Nicholas and his son, Tsesarevich Alexander.

"Your Imperial Majesties."

"Countess Markova." Nicholas beamed, offering her his arm. "My dear, so good to see you again."

"I'm sorry I've been absent of late, Your Imperial Majesty," she said. She did like Nicholas, though she thought his ideas on the Oriental War wrong. "How is our dear tsarina?"

"Her health does not improve," he said, shaking his head. His voice took on a heavy sadness, and she knew, despite his long affair with Barbara Nelidova, he truly loved his wife. Katria wondered if she could accept Nikolai being with another.

No. The answer was quick, decisive. She'd kill the other woman first.

Dismissing these thoughts, she continued to look for Nikolai to no avail. Did he purposely avoid her because of their last conversation?

The tsesarevich joined them, and Katria noticed Pavel trailing behind them. Her betrothed looked anything but pleased, but neither the tsar nor his son seemed inclined to include him in their conversation. Katria certainly didn't wish to.

Alexander's heavy mustache twitched with mirth as he watched Pavel from the corner of his eye. "And you, Countess? I heard of your brother's disappearance." The mustache stilled and a frown marred his already-lined face.

"Yes," she murmured. Katria didn't look at Pavel, and wondered if he was involved in the attack on Constantine or if it was solely Sergey's doing. "I hope he's found, and I hope he lives. Father is less optimistic."

The tsesarevich nodded, and Nicholas patted her hand. "I'm sure everything that can be done to discover his whereabouts is being done."

Nodding, Katria changed the subject. She wanted to continue speaking with both of them for a bit longer. "I'm sure," she said and hoped the derision she felt wasn't heard in her voice, "you know my fiancé?"

Pavel, like a trained dog, stepped forward. She marveled he hadn't drunk his own glass of champagne, and pointed so the footman would approach the tsar.

"Your Imperial Majesty." He bowed. Though he looked as if he wanted to say more, he didn't, standing there awkwardly as the tsar took a glass and downed its contents in one swallow.

"I've convinced Father to wait until Constantine's situation is determined," Katria said, once more ignoring Pavel. "I want my brother at my wedding."

Pavel sputtered for a moment, but didn't contradict her. Offering Nicholas a brilliant smile, she bowed to Alexander, then to the tsar.

"If you'll excuse us, Your Imperial Majesties."

They nodded as she backed away, Pavel at her side. Her fingers twisted in the lace at the side of her gown as she wandered through the Great Hall, where she spotted Anatoli.

Kissing her uncle's cheek, she waited as Pavel completed the ritual greeting. Anatoli stood through it patiently, blessing him without a hint of irony. Pavel, on the other hand, seemed less than enthused, almost resentful that he had to bow before the bishop.

"Uncle," she greeted Anatoli. "The wedding was lovely, and the chapel is always gorgeous." She nodded at the crowd. "I'm surprised at the number in attendance this evening. It seems all of St. Petersburg is here."

"Indeed," Anatoli agreed, taking her arm and slipping her hand through his elbow. "It's quite stifling. With your permission," he said to Pavel though he already turned away from the man, "I'd like to take my niece for a stroll."

"Of course, Your Grace." Pavel didn't look pleased, but neither Katria nor Anatoli cared and had already started walking away when he bowed.

"If you require anything else," he offered as they walked eastward along the windows from the Great Hall through the Concert Hall. As they passed the life-sized statues of the nine muses of ancient Greece, he added, "All you need to do is ask."

Passing numerous couples, ladies in waiting, old dowagers sitting in the red brocade-covered chairs, she shook her head. Nikolai remained elusive, though she sensed he watched her.

"I don't believe so, Uncle."

"I'm surprised you restrained yourself, Katria," he said, ignoring a wave from a cluster of ladies standing by the floor-to-ceiling windows.

"It was not easy," she admitted as they wandered into the Malachite Room.

The crowd was gone here, the guests of the Ulensky wedding moving between rooms of the Neva Enfilade. The private retreat, used by the Imperial family during official functions, and where the Romanov brides traditionally dressed before their own weddings, was often off limits to the nobility. However, Anatoli nodded to the guards and they allowed them to pass.

"But I found that to have Father under my control," she continued as she gazed around the room, "rather than to cause another death was more advantageous."

She'd never been in this room, but it was as beautiful as she'd heard. The green malachite columns glistened in the afternoon sunlight, and the gold accents only highlighted the grandeur of the malachite. No wonder the tsars kept it to themselves.

Anatoli nodded. "I can see your logic and agree with you. However, should temperaments change, do not hesitate to protect yourself."

"I shan't, Uncle."

He turned, leading her back to the Great Hall. "The next stage of our plan has gone smoothly." Nodding to the guards, he steered them to the crowd of ladies who had waved him over earlier. "We must ensure it moves smoothly until the end," he whispered.

As they bowed in ritual greeting, Katria spotted Nikolai. As she'd anticipated, he wasn't far. Stalking her in the shadow of the guests, she imagined. She'd worn this gown, with its unusual shade of blue, the color of ice, so he could easily track her through the hall. It wouldn't do to lose sight of each other now.

To her disappointment, Pavel rejoined her and Anatoli. The women her uncle was speaking with noticed his repugnant stare and commented in whisper. "You are so fortunate to have such an attentive fiancé."

****

The way he looked at her aggravated each of Nikolai's senses. He observed Katria and Pavel from across the Great Hall and wanted to rip the man's arms off. Thumbing his glass, he wondered just how disturbed the tsar would be if he broke off the stem of the glass and impaled Pavel Radoff here, in view of the entire wedding party.

He supposed it might cause some trouble. *Might* being the operative word. With the few friends Pavel had, it could possibly go unnoticed. Nikolai couldn't help but smile at the thought.

Soon enough.

"Orlov."

Nikolai turned to see Princess Ulensky approach and eyed her suspiciously.

"I'm happy to see you chose to attend," the old bat said graciously. "You cannot allow all those nasty rumors that spread about your brother to affect you. I heard they were cruel lies spread by those who sought to advance themselves. It's a tricky game we play here."

Fully aware that Ulensky had been among the first to jump atop the rumors, Nikolai decided to accept her oblique olive branch. She was a shrewd woman who could prove valuable in the future. "It is, Princess. Some play this game better than others, and I dare say you are one of the finer players."

With a wide grin, Ulensky acknowledged the compliment. "It's good to have fresh blood in the Palace. Pay no mind to the false tales, Orlov. They will vanish swiftly." She inclined her head to the room. "The moment they scent a fresh corpse."

"If only that corpse could be Pavel Radoff," he mused, eyeing her as he did so.

Ulenksy scowled at the name. Nikolai hid a smile. "Viktor did you great harm when he dissolved your engagement. The action lent credence to the lies surrounding Peter," the Princess stated. "But they are not wed yet, Nikolai," she added with a cunning smile. "The tide could always shift in your favor."

"With your assistance, perhaps it will." He offered her a sensuous smile and watched as it softened her hardened core.

"What can I do?" the older woman inquired.

****

The ride home from the Palace was intolerably quiet. Katria would have preferred it if Pavel had continued his taunts. Instead, he just watched her in such a covetous way, she wished to bathe immediately.

The trim on the side of her gown was, in all probability, ravaged by her fingers. Smoothing the lace, Katria wondered how Constantine fared. She hadn't heard anything about his health in days, and while she knew Anna tended him, she still needed to see him for herself. Damn Anatoli for refusing to take her to him. He was her brother, and no matter the danger to both her and Constantine, she needed to see him.

Pavel's eyes continued to watch her, and she stilled her fingers. Oh, for the day she could be rid of him. Again, Katria reminded herself this was partly her idea.

The carriage halted and she exited before the footman could open the door. She couldn't spend another moment with Pavel. He followed her to the house.

"Really, there's no need to see me in," she said, turning on the top step. Her butler opened the door and she nodded to him, stalling Pavel.

"Of course there is," he insisted and barged into the house.

Grimacing, Katria followed him in, handing her cloak to the butler. The man nodded and she entered the front parlor where Pavel had already poured himself a glass of vodka.

"Have I told you what a beautiful dress that is?" he asked, toasting her. "The cut flatters you nicely. I especially like the way it molds to your breasts."

Disgusted, she turned to call the butler and have Pavel forcibly thrown out.

"I'd like to see what's under that gown. As we're engaged..." His hand was on her arm before she crossed the threshold into the foyer. Spinning her, he finished, "There's no need to wait."

"I warned you."

Nikolai's voice cut through the room like a gunshot. Pavel stiffened, his hand convulsing on her arm. Katria smiled at him, a satisfied twist of her lips. Pavel released her with a cry as Nikolai wrenched his arm behind his back.

"You still can't do anything to me, Orlov," Pavel managed through gritted teeth.

"Don't worry," Nikolai promised in a low voice. "I won't kill you. I'll barely leave a mark."

"Anything you do to me," Pavel spat, "I'll see on Katria tenfold. You won't always be here to protect her. She'll be *mine*, not yours. And I intend to treat her as such."

"If you live that long."

Katria watched the exchange, wondering at Nikolai's ability to keep himself in check. The tension coming off him showed her how much he wanted to harm Pavel.

"We're not married yet," she said to Pavel as Nikolai propelled him to the front door. "We shall see if it comes to pass."

Opening the door so Nikolai could toss Pavel into the street, Katria ignored her intended's stammerings. Slamming the door behind him, she turned to Nikolai and grinned.

"Missed you," she said and launched herself into his arms.

Chapter Seventeen

February 27, 1855
Georgian Calendar

NIKOLAI WATCHED her sleep. He hadn't really had the chance to do that before, and hadn't realized how much he wanted to. Katria lay across the bed, long hair wild over his pillows. He refused to let her return to Viktor's house, no matter what damage to her reputation staying the night with him might cause.

He trusted Katria when she said she had her father well in hand, but he trusted Viktor about as much as a Russian wolf in the cold of winter.

She shifted, one hand reaching out for him. Not finding him, she rolled over, snuggling into the depression his body made in the mattress.

Pushing off from the wall where he leaned naked, Nikolai sat on the edge of the bed. Stroking her hair, he wondered if this was the right direction. Yes, it made sense to clear his name, to destroy those responsible for Peter's death and Constantine's attack. But Katria was far from safe.

Pavel had nearly raped her this afternoon.

His fingers convulsed in her hair, and he deliberately relaxed them. Defending herself with words and politics was one thing, but her strength was no match for Pavel's.

"I'm going to kill him," he promised her sleeping form.

Protecting her was all that mattered now. He had told her the truth when he said he didn't care about his reputation, about his family's name, about Alexey. His uncle and family could fend for themselves. Katria was all that mattered.

She hadn't said she loved him. Before he had admitted his own love for her, Nikolai didn't think he needed to hear her return the sentiment. But he did. Beyond reason, beyond logic and thought, he loved her. Needed her. The shell she wore had originally attracted him, but the passion she hid beneath it had made for an irresistible challenge.

She had made him love her.

Sighing, he stood. He was thinking like a foolish Russian poet. Or worse, an English one. Stalking through the room, uncaring of his nakedness, he thought about the next stage of their plan.

But first, he had promised to take her to visit Constantine. What story Anatoli circulated as to Countess Tiomkin's whereabouts, Nikolai hadn't yet heard. But so long as she remained with his friend, he knew Constantine was safe.

"Come back to bed."

Her voice was hoarse from sleep. Nikolai turned to see her, head propped on one hand, the other stretched toward him. He crossed the room in quick strides, pulling her up to kneel on the bed.

"I didn't want to wake you."

"It no fun sleeping in the bed alone," she teased, her mouth kissing down his neck. An eager pupil, Katria seemed fascinated with his body, constantly tasting and touching. He wasn't about to discourage her exploration.

"If you insist on keeping me here and ruining my reputation," she said, fingers digging into his shoulder to tug him onto the bed, "you should at least have the courtesy to keep me warm."

The fact the fire continued to blaze in the fireplace meant nothing. "I'm sorry to be so remiss in my duties," he said, kissing her shoulder and tugging her nipple.

"You're forgiven," she gasped, arching into him.

Laying her on the bed, Nikolai spread her dark hair across the white sheets. He took his time, savoring every taste of her flesh, every moan and cry from her lips. Her hands, small and warm, glided over his chest, across shoulders and down his back to press him further into her. She eagerly touched him on his hips and down his thighs.

Lifting her onto her knees, her back to his front, he spread her legs, dipped a finger into her and felt her tighten around him, his mouth tasting along her neck. She twisted slightly, found his mouth with hers and feasted. He loved kissing her, loved the way her tongue felt against his, her moist breath mingled with his, lips pressed against lips.

He withdrew his finger to tease her nipples, tugging on the hardened points until she shuddered. Spreading her legs wider, Katria leaned forward and thrust back against him. Nikolai could feel her wetness, but held off entering her. He wasn't quite ready.

Running his fingers down her belly, over her ribs, stroking her hipbone, he teased her wet folds with light caresses that hinted at what he wanted to do to her. He caught her gasp of breath with his lips, refusing to release her. His fingers trailed back up her body, heated both from him and the fire, to capture her hard nipples, once more twisting them just as she liked.

She shuddered harder now, teetering on the precipice of orgasm.

"Nikolai," she whispered, head falling to his shoulder, grinding insistently against him.

He turned her, settling her over him. Katria's legs locked around his hips, and she whimpered his name, the sound turning into a cry of need when Nikolai finally entered her.

Their pace was slow and savoring, gasps of pleasure filling the air at every movement, every caress. Then they were moving faster, harder, straining for that peak that would bring them the ultimate bliss. Crying out his name, Katria clenched around Nikolai, her orgasm crashing through her. Scant moments later, Nikolai stiffened in release, her name echoing around the room before he collapsed atop his lover.

Running a soothing hand through his hair and down his back, Katria held him to her. Eventually Nikolai rolled over, cradling her in his arms as they drifted to sleep.

****

"Uncle," Katria said from across the table where they enjoyed their luncheon.

It was two days after the Palace wedding. Katria hadn't returned to Viktor's house, sending only a servant to fetch more clothes for her. They'd been careful to prevent her from being seen outside the townhouse, mindful of her reputation and her public engagement to Radoff.

With Tiomkin watching over Constantine, and the rumor she'd taken ill spreading through court, it was simple enough to pretend Katria visited her sick friend. No one would question it, and Anna's parents perpetuated the rumor. Apparently, Anatoli trusted them enough to bring them into the secret.

Anatoli sat there and looked the perfect bishop, not letting the obvious fact his niece spent the night with Nikolai aggravate him. Nikolai, uncaring what he thought about their sleeping arrangements, chewed a forkful of pork.

"Have your servants acquired the information we need?"

Nodding, Anatoli said, "I believe we have everything. However, I understand Sergey sequesters himself in residence for several days, so we have until tomorrow night." He slanted a glance in Nikolai's direction. "I'm told it's his habit after a Palace function."

"Then we should visit him," Katria smiled.

"I don't want you going there alone," Nikolai said.

"She won't be," Anatoli interjected. "With Anna's illness, I've agreed to accompany her."

Nikolai scowled. The old man had more than revenge against the Radoffs up his sleeve, he knew it. *What*, though, was the question.

Grunting, he acknowledged, "I suppose if I accompany you myself, you won't get far."

For a moment, Katria studied him, then laughed, a light, happy sound that warmed him and lessened his concern about her being in Radoff's house. Just a little, but enough to bring a smile to his face.

"With a few discreet questions to Radoff," Anatoli said, "I should be able to discern his movements for the next few days."

"I'm certain I'll be able to track Pavel." She shuddered, and Nikolai's fingers fisted around his fork. "He isn't exactly subtle."

Deliberately changing the subject before he and Katria got into another argument, Nikolai asked, "How is Tsar Nicholas?"

"He worsens." Anatoli frowned. He looked concerned and shook his head. "I fear it's more than a winter's cold. The physicians will attend to him, however, his illness is the perfect reason to drop in on Sergey."

****

Antsy, Katria bounced her leg as the carriage slid through the freshly fallen snow. They'd just left his townhouse, and Anatoli had promised to wait for them there.

"Relax," Nikolai said, squeezing her hand. "We'll be there shortly."

"I know."

He didn't want her to worry, though he was consumed with anxiety. Constantine had looked better yesterday than when he'd seen him three days ago, and Nikolai trusted his health had much improved since then. She turned to smile at him, but she kept her hand in his.

"Shot, concussed, under the frozen waters of the Neva for who knows how long…" Katria's voice trailed off.

"He's strong, Katria," Nikolai promised as the carriage rounded the last corner. Anatoli had installed the recuperating Constantine across St. Petersburg, in a small house on the border between the prosperous and seedy sides of town. It was sufficiently distant from court, yet wouldn't be too suspicious when a carriage arrived.

"Is he still feverish?" she asked.

"Yes," Nikolai said patiently, although it was the fourth time she had asked. "But Tiomkin cares for him and sees that the best doctors tend him."

"He's safe?" she asked.

Her foot continued to tap, the fingers of her free hand twisting in her skirts. The carriage slid to a halt, shaking as the driver descended. Nikolai removed his hand and gently tugged the hood of her cloak around her face, pressing his lips to hers. He'd thought about hiring a carriage to take them instead of using his own, but dismissed it as an unnecessary precaution.

The fewer people who knew they traveled across town together, the better, and a hired carriage driver was never trustworthy.

"Safe as can be," he said as the door opened and he exited to help her down. "The doctor removed the bullet and sewed him up. The freezing waters from the Neva prevented the wound from bleeding excessively."

Katria shuddered, and for a moment, Nikolai wondered whether he'd said too much. But no, she nodded and took his offered arm.

"He'll be well," she whispered.

The door opened and they entered the dimly lit foyer. The air smelled stale and sick, though Nikolai noticed several windows open in the parlor. Anna Tiomkin stood in the shadows, her gown wrinkled and stained. Katria embraced her.

"Thank you," she said, squeezing her friend's hands. "Where is he?"

"Upstairs." Anna nodded toward the steps. "He's still feverish, but less so."

Katria turned to look at him, and Nikolai nodded. This was her private time with Constantine, though he did follow her into the room.

Constantine lay propped up on several pillows, eyes closed, seemingly oblivious to his surroundings. Katria sat on the bed and took his hand.

"Constantine?" she said softly. He didn't stir.

To Anna, Nikolai asked, "Has he said anything?"

"About what happened?" She shook her head. "No. He's regained consciousness several times, but the fever saps his strength. The doctors are not hopeful."

Katria whispered to her brother, and Nikolai would have given half his estates to know what she said. After she turned to look at him over her shoulder, he would have given the other half. Since the breaking of their engagement, she'd seemed different. The woman he'd sought to discover was still there, yet Nikolai sensed her closing off once more.

When they were in bed, she was open, passionate, everything he knew her to be. Yet in the harsh light of day, even a Russian winter's day, she again retreated behind her protective wall.

"Is there anything you require?" he asked Anna.

"No, His Grace provides all I may need and sends a messenger over twice a day."

Nikolai nodded and wondered if she needed more than Anatoli could provide, but didn't offer. There was a reason he'd picked Anna, one he'd not seen fit to share with Nikolai. What did he know of Anna Tiomkin the rest of them did not? What did she and her family provide to Anatoli?

"Katria?"

Constantine's voice cut through the room.

Anna took an involuntary step forward, but Nikolai held her back. Katria leaned closer, smoothing a cold cloth over Constantine's brow. His head lolled in her direction, his eyes struggling to open.

More whispering, but this time Nikolai interrupted. He'd have given her the rest of the day, but he didn't want to lose this opportunity with Constantine.

"Constantine," he said. With his hand on Katria's shoulder, he leaned over her. One of her soft hands left her brother's and took his, squeezing it. Nikolai held it tight. "Do you know who did this?"

"Terenov," Constantine's weak voice whispered through the room. "I'm not positive, but it had to be him."

"We know." Nikolai nodded, hoping for more. "He's been taken care of."

Eyes already closed, Constantine nodded his understanding, once more drifting into his fevered sleep.

Katria leaned forward, kissed his cheek, and rested her head on his chest for a long moment. She never released his hand, and when she stood, Nikolai noticed tears in the brilliant blue-green depths of her eyes. She shook herself and blinked the tears away.

To Anna she said, "Thank you."

Leading her out, Nikolai offered, "The doctor thinks he'll recover."

"Thank you," she said as she stepped into the carriage. There, she leaned her head against his chest and he held her as she silently sobbed.

****

"Damn peasants are never timely," Pavel muttered. He stood in the bitter winds adjusting his heavy fur-lined greatcoat. In the less desirable part of St. Petersburg, he paced by the river.

Pavel hated to wait. If he was home with a drink in hand or at the Palace, where a multitude of other little diversions kept him occupied, he didn't mind. But waiting anywhere else, and for a servant much less, irritated him beyond reason.

It didn't, however, bother him more than Nikolai Orlov did. The man was a pariah who needed to be eliminated. Threatening him, trying to dictate how he behaved around his own woman. And Katria was indeed *his woman*.

Orlov lost, yet he wouldn't go away.

"Excellency?" a voice sounded behind him.

Pavel turned to face the man. He was older than he expected and slimmer, hunched against the wind. But, Pavel supposed, as long as he could wield a knife, he'd do. "I've been waiting."

"This is the time I was told to appear here," the man responded, his hands hidden in the pockets of his ragged wool coat.

"You need to learn to anticipate." Pavel's disdain was clear in his tone. "Here." He shoved a small piece of paper toward the man. "Here's the address, should you be literate." The man took the paper and nodded. Pavel had his doubts about that. "Should you be illiterate, there's a map on the other side." Pavel scowled. "Kill Count Nikolai Orlov. Do it quickly, but it does *not* have to be painless."

"And the pay?" the man asked as he took the scrap of paper.

"Once I know it has been accomplished," he said, "I'll meet you back here and you'll receive your compensation."

"Is there any way you could see to giving me some now?" he whined. "Excellency?"

This man was pathetic. Was this the best he could do to rid himself of Orlov? Pavel didn't even want to consider what his father would say about this hire. He could hear the old man's voice lecturing him now.

"You won't receive a single ruble until I know Orlov is dead." Pavel scowled at him, left the man standing by the river and headed back to the relative warmth of his carriage.

Chapter Eighteen

"I'M NOT sure what I was expecting," Katria commented as she and Anatoli waited in the Radoffs' foyer. Neither of them had ever set foot in the Radoff home before, and now she unobtrusively looked around. "Perhaps I expected to see stolen Palace furniture lining the halls."

"I admit I had the same thought." Anatoli's laugh was low.

"As far as I can tell, everything is very well appointed. That landscape painting," Katria stated as she nodded to a large rural landscape gracing the far wall. "It's stunning. Seems Finnish, perhaps Magnus von Wright?"

The room was elegant without being ostentatious. Small brocade-covered settees circled the rounded foyer, and a cut-crystal chandelier hung high over the marble floor. She'd never have guessed Sergey, much less Pavel, resided in such an elegant atmosphere.

Anatoli tugged Katria's arm as the butler returned for them. Her eyes traveled the room, over vases, paintings, silver sconces, curious as to what lay behind each door.

They entered the parlor to find Sergey with book in hand. "Your Grace. Countess. What a pleasant surprise." Sergey rose to greet Anatoli properly and moved to kiss Katria's hand. She was reluctant to offer it but did—she still wasn't certain it would be returned to her in one piece.

"I've come with Katria to discuss the wedding," Anatoli began as they all moved to the seating area.

"I know Pavel is anxious for the ceremony. I hope you've managed to secure the Palace chapel?" Sergey waited for Katria to take her seat. He gestured to the sideboard, but she shook her head. "Katria, I know the Ulensky wedding was a triumph, and such a guest list! But I don't think we'll be able to gather such a distinguished crowd in the short time we have."

"Princess Ulensky planned her daughter's wedding for near on a year," Katria offered as she smoothed her skirt. She looked up at him with an innocent expression. "Anything remotely on that scale would be impossible."

"Never say impossible, child." Sergey good-naturedly scolded her. Katria found his humor slightly alarming. She wanted to swallow her words as he sat opposite her and Anatoli, clearly thinking over what she had said. "A good majority of Ulensky's attendees are still in St. Petersburg," he mused. "I'm sure the tsar would relish another lavish wedding to divert his attention from the recent battles."

"The tsar has taken ill," Anatoli said.

"I had heard he had a winter cold." Sergey nodded. "A few days abed should right our emperor."

"I've come with concern about the tsar's health, and to ask that Katria and Pavel's wedding be postponed until after Lent." Anatoli leaned back in his seat, hands folded over his chest; the appearance of one not to be crossed.

"I'm an old man, Your Grace," Sergey said. "Must I wait an even longer time than needed for a grandchild?" He glanced at Katria and she wanted to vomit. "And such a beautiful child it shall be."

Smiling through the nausea she felt at the mere thought of Pavel touching her, Katria stood. "Count Radoff, I would like a bit of air. Please excuse me."

It wasn't how she'd intended to leave his company, but his comment had ruined her carefully planned conversation.

"Of course," he said smoothly, standing to gesture out the doors. "Tour the house, Katria. You need to familiarize yourself with your home and this is a perfect opportunity."

With a nod to Radoff, Katria left the parlor to find herself in the foyer. Behind her, she heard Anatoli say, "Her brother's...*disappearance* causes her great sadness. She had hoped he would attend her wedding when the time came."

"Now," she whispered to herself as she stepped out of view of the parlor doors. "Which room would be used the least?"

Hurrying down the hall, she silently opened each door she encountered: dining room, a study and library, the ballroom. *Perhaps the ballroom*, she thought, though she wasn't fond of the locale.

Then she opened the door to the music room. Entering, she glanced about the vast space. The mahogany piano gleamed, a golden harp stood in one corner, and a sideboard held two violins. There wasn't a speck of dust to be found, and the wear on the piano's pedals was slight.

This is the perfect room.

Sergey and Pavel seemed to enter here rarely; only the servants came in and out to keep it clean. Leaning out the door, she glanced up and down the hall to ensure it remained empty. Closing the doors with a soft click, she debated the best place to hide her evidence.

Katria pulled a folded sheet of paper free from her bodice and went to the fireplace. The paper had been purposely singed in one corner, and she needed to place that end closest to the fire. She moved the screen and reached in. Immediately finding just the right spot, she slid the paper up and between the bricks. Taking great care not to soil her dress, she wedged it in place.

After moving the screen back into place, she retrieved her handkerchief and wiped off the black smudges on her fingers.

With a last deep breath, she exited the room and returned to Radoff and Anatoli. Their plan was in motion.

****

"Anatoli dropped me off," she said, closing the door behind her.

Nikolai supposed he should worry about her reputation; she slept in his house these last nights, sending her maid to fetch clothing and other items she needed. No matter how discreet they were, there were sure to be rumors circulating around the Palace. Nikolai didn't care. He was worried about her *life* if she were left in Viktor's house.

And he enjoyed waking next to her, making love to her all night and sleeping with her in his arms.

"Why was your trip so lengthy?" he asked. "Every moment you're in that house, I worry."

Which was an understatement. Jealousy speared through him all the time she spent away from him. Unreasonable though it was, he couldn't help it. That, and he really wanted to kill Pavel. Sergey Radoff, too, for what he'd done to his family, but Pavel for daring to touch Katria.

"Everything went smoothly, Nikolai." She smiled. But there was a hardness in her voice he hated. He knew he was responsible for it. "I accomplished my task."

"Good. You've accomplished everything you needed to," Nikolai said as evenly as he could manage. "Now that you have Viktor under your influence, the time has come to end your engagement with Radoff."

"I disagree," she said. They circled each other as they used to, half a room apart; dancing around each other and the topic at hand. "We may still use this association to our advantage."

"I don't see any further use for Pavel," he said.

"Nikolai," she soothed, "you're reacting emotionally. You must look at this with logic."

"I look at everything logically, Katria," he said, stalking forward until she backed against the wall. "And logic dictates that I remove you from the vipers' nest as quickly as possible."

Tossing her head, Katria skirted to the side, out of his reach. Not running, purposely avoiding. Her eyes narrowed, brilliant jewels in the gas-lit bedroom.

"How dare you?" she asked. "I've managed my safety well enough. Have I not?'

"You've managed admirably, love," he agreed. He tracked her, but didn't attempt to corner her again. "But you're still young, and still unaware of all the varied ways they can harm you."

Her hands fisted, then loosened in the skirts of her gown, and she took an angry step forward. "You've no idea what I've already had to deal with," she said. "I can handle whatever I have to in order to accomplish my goal."

"And what goal is that?"

But it wasn't a question. He didn't need an answer to understand her. Nikolai realized, his heart breaking, exactly what she meant. Katria retreated from him, stepping back emotionally as she refused to do physically. Oh, she'd fight to the bitter end, but she'd do so from behind that perfect wall she had so carefully constructed.

"My goal," she said through her teeth, anger the only emotion breaking through her barrier, "is to get everything I want."

His blood froze. Vigilant about showing how that stabbed him, he asked in a deliberately lazy voice, "Not what *we* want?"

"Not if you keep trying to dominate me, Nikolai," she retorted. "I don't take kindly to being penned in. I always find a way to set myself free."

Snapping, Nikolai stalked forward. Katria tried to skirt him again, but he would have none of it. Grabbing her by the arms, he snarled, "Don't do this. Don't retreat from all the progress we've made. The emotional progress."

He didn't want to shake her, but he couldn't keep his own feelings in check. He loved her. He needed her. And he'd be damned if he'd let her, of all people, come between what he knew they shared.

"I had you. I had all of you. And I have no intention of letting you go."

Katria shrugged off his hands and whirled away. "You don't understand!" she shouted. "It's not your choice!"

"Katria—"

"I'm under no one's thumb!" Her voice cracked even as it rang with defiance.

She picked up the closest item she could find, the gas lamp, and hurled it at him. He dodged it, following its progress as it crashed into the wall. The floor caught on fire. Grabbing his discarded jacket from the high-backed chair, Nikolai smothered the flames before they could do more than singe a hole in the carpet.

Composing himself, he looked at the mess on the floor. The spilled kerosene, the splintered glass, the ruined carpet, the scorched hardwood beneath; he cared nothing for it.

He'd lost her.

Slowly, he turned, fingers still gripping the ruined jacket. Could he go through with their marriage? Could he marry her knowing he loved her beyond all reason and she—she didn't love him? Nikolai had hoped. He'd believed she had. Beneath her prickly exterior, he still believed she loved him. Or cared for him enough to love him. He had to believe it was more than mutual lust.

Facing her, knowing this was the end, Nikolai was surprised to see the naked fear on her face. One hand covered her mouth and she stared with wide eyes at the floor.

"I'm sorry." The words were quiet, but in the aftermath of their fight, they sounded deafening. She backed away, her eyes moving from the floor to him, her hand still covering her mouth. "I'm sorry."

Damnation.

Striding across the room, Nikolai dropped his jacket. Before he could stop her, she fled. As she ran down the stairs, he swore he heard her sob. Taking the steps two at a time, he reached her before she could do more than open the door.

One hand slammed it closed, and the other turned her to face him.

"You're free, Nikolai. Forget about this," she said, backing away. "Forget about us. We'll exact our revenge on the Radoffs, but we can't do this. We can't do us."

Pulling her into his arms, he didn't release her no matter how she struggled. He wanted to shake her but didn't. Wanted to tell her, *no, never, he couldn't ever forget her*, but words failed him. All he could do was hold her as she tried to push him away.

Utterly calm, he pulled back. "I'm not letting you go."

"I'm damaged, Nikolai."

Fighting him, she struggled to open the door to leave. Pinning her arms to her side, he rested his forehead against hers.

"I am too."

With measured movements, she pulled back and watched him. Unmoving for long moments, she just stood there. Loosening his hold on her, Nikolai waited. Her hand hovered over his cheek, not touching it. Then she dropped it.

Catching her fingers, he brought her hand to his lips. Kissing the palm, he nodded. "Without you, there'd be nothing left inside me."

A single tear fell down her cheek. Brushing it away, he said, "Come to bed, Katria. Don't leave."

Chapter Nineteen

March 2, 1855
Georgian Calendar

TSAR NICHOLAS I was dead. Constantine waited while the driver jumped down and opened the door. The old man helped him out, carefully walking him to the front doorway, Anatoli trailing behind. Nodding his thanks, he tipped the man, another one loyal to Anatoli.

Leaning heavily on his cane, Constantine thought about his emperor's death. His cold had turned deadly in a matter of days and he'd succumbed early this dreary morning. Or at least that's what Anatoli had told him when he'd brought fresh clothes this afternoon and dismissed Anna.

Anna. Katria's friend proved to be more than another simple courtier. He'd wanted to question why she tended him, but hadn't the strength. Even now, as the butler opened the door, gaping at him as if he saw a ghost, Constantine could barely walk into the townhouse.

Viktor sat behind his desk, his head in his hands, no doubt planning his next political move. By rights, he should've already been at the Palace, and yet here he sat. Constantine wondered where Katria was; Anatoli had been suspiciously mum as to her whereabouts.

"Good Afternoon, Father."

Viktor twitched, and he slowly raised his head. Pale, he stared between Constantine and Anatoli. "What's this?"

"Your son," Anatoli said somewhat dryly.

"Thank you for the warm and gracious welcome, Father." Constantine took a step into the study. His breath was short and his knees threatened to betray him, but he refused to tremble and show Viktor how weak he truly was.

"We'll be spending much time together from here on out," he said wryly. "I've dispatched a footman to the Palace to inform them of my miraculous return, in the event you had planned anything."

Cornered, Viktor paused in the act of rising. Whatever he had planned, he could no longer get away with it—the new tsar knew of his whereabouts.

"We'll have plenty to talk about—I'm not returning to the military."

"Constantine," Viktor managed. His son didn't give him the chance to say more.

"I'm retiring to my former rooms to rest," he informed the other man. He paused and added, "Aside from Katria and her friend, Anna, I don't wish to be disturbed by anyone."

Anatoli watched his nephew climb the stairs, leaning heavily on a footman. Turning to his brother, he said, "You've heard of the tsar's death?"

Viktor nodded numbly. Usually, Anatoli expected a crass retort, because Viktor prided himself on always knowing the latest news. Now, his older brother looked ill.

"The illness came on too quickly," he said. "I find it unusual how his illness progressed."

That got Viktor's attention and his head snapped around. With a nod, Anatoli left. He had much to see to this day.

****

Katria didn't want to open her eyes. Cocooned in the warmth of Nikolai's embrace, his hands gently stroking her arms, she wanted to indulge in his body. He'd held her thus all night, hands possessive through the chemisette she wore. The room smelled of strong cleaner; the servants had unobtrusively cleaned the kerosene from the floor downstairs. They'd been quick about it, too.

She shifted, felt his pants-covered leg with her foot. He grunted behind her, a soft puff of breath tickling her ear. Trailing her fingers along his arm, she stretched.

"I love you."

Somewhat surprised the words didn't stick in her throat, Katria felt the truth of them. She loved him. It wasn't just that he didn't abandon her when she tried to kill him with the gas lamp, either. What she felt for Nikolai was deep and true, and she could no longer deny it.

Since the moment they met, it was everything. From his persistence to his possessiveness, even. The way he looked at her, the way he touched her. How he listened to her about everything, from her planning to her sillier moments, and stood beside her.

She loved how this dangerous man softened in her presence. He'd shown her love the entire time and it wasn't until last night that she'd accepted it. Completely, entirely accepted it. Katria knew she'd spent too much time surviving the machinations of others. It was that experience that made it so hard to recognize the truth in Nikolai's eyes.

Turning over, she kissed him awake. His arms tightened around her, as if he thought she might be an illusion.

"Katria."

"I love you, Nikolai."

He stilled and pulled back. For a heartbeat, she thought she was too late, but then he pulled her closer, his mouth hard on hers, hungry.

Her mouth throbbing from his kiss, Katria whimpered when he held her at arm's length, watching her. It was a long, hard look, inscrutable.

"I believe you."

Relief swept through her. Taking his hand, she kissed the back of it.

"I love you," he said.

Not thinking, not analyzing, Katria kissed him. Her hands combed through his short hair, over his naked shoulders, down his back. Unbuttoning his trousers, she fought to undress him while they still lay in bed. Nikolai laughed against her mouth, tugging her chemisette over her head, kissing down her neck.

Emboldened by her admission, Katria pressed against his chest, her fingers digging into the hard muscle there. Forcing him flat on his back, she straddled him. His fingers found her nipples, tugging until she cried out. She wanted to taste him, wanted to spend the rest of the day discovering everything about him.

He entered her in one quick movement. It was the most exquisite feeling she could imagine. How he filled her, their connection, was earth-shattering. Rocking against him, she moved faster. His hands moved along the curve of her back, over her hips, gripping them as he slammed into her.

"Nikolai!" she cried out when he flipped her, hands holding her thigh against him.

Straining for that delicious peak, she sobbed in frustration as his hands outlined the circle of her breasts. Writhing beneath him, she moved her legs higher, arching her hips to bring him deeper into her.

Passion pounded through her, and she forgot all save the need of him. His fingers found her, and Katria screamed his name as waves of ecstasy thrummed through her. The degree to which she responded was even more intense than before.

Nikolai thrust again, his mouth clamping on her neck as he, too, found release.

She loved this man. Her heart, soul, and every other bit of her loved this man.

"We'll marry as soon as the tsar allows it," she whispered, curling into his side, her head resting on his chest.

His laugh rumbled under her ear.

****

Nikolai assisted her into the carriage. The day was bleak, overcast; another threat of snow hung over a city weeping for its emperor. When he and Katria finally emerged from their bedroom, it was to discover the house in mourning, the mantels and banisters draped in black. Tsar Nicholas I was dead.

It all happened so quickly.

A hand seized his left arm, turning him. The knife glinted in the weak light, and before Nikolai could react, the man plunged the dagger into him. It skidded along his back, off the gun he carried at his hip.

Punching the man before he had the chance to strike again, Nikolai wrenched his coat open and pulled out his gun. Leveling it on the other man, he paused. But his attacker lunged. Nikolai shot him in the chest.

There was an immediate crowd around the carriage. Katria tried to descend the steps, but he pushed her back in the carriage.

"I'm all right," he whispered, pressing his mouth quickly to hers. To his driver he called, "Drive!"

The carriage's sleighs hastened over the snow as one man checked the neck of the attacker. "A robbery," he declared, "in the middle of the afternoon! And on a day we all mourn."

He shook his head, asking Nikolai a lot of unnecessary questions. Fire burned through his side, but he didn't move.

That hadn't been a robbery. That had been an assassination attempt.

****

Anatoli didn't bother to halt Katria's pacing. The court barely noticed her movements, anyway. From the story she related to him about the attack on Nikolai, he believed she had ample cause to worry.

Nikolai bounded up the staircase and cut through the crowd. Anatoli breathed a sigh of relief.

"How does the tsar's death affect our plans?" Nikolai asked the instant he joined them.

Katria stood at his side, worried eyes raking his body. But she said nothing and, thank God, didn't rush into his arms.

"I'm uncertain," Anatoli admitted with a frown. "We may have to reevaluate how we proceed."

"I want to break off my engagement with Pavel, Uncle," Katria said.

Nodding in relief, Anatoli pointed to where Viktor spoke with several other ministers. "Speak with your father. I'll arrange things on my end."

He waited as she squeezed Nikolai's hand and the younger man's gaze followed her. "Is she well?" he demanded.

"Yes." Nikolai smiled. "She truly is."

Worried her breaking point was near with all that had occurred this past month, Anatoli was pleased to learn her health had not declined. He truly loved the girl and wanted her to be happy. With Nikolai, she was. She loved Orlov; there was no doubt in Anatoli's mind.

Since she was young, he had wanted this for her: to escape Viktor's house and have the life she deserved. Satisfied with Nikolai's answer, Anatoli waited while Katria returned.

"The engagement is off," she said. "Father didn't even object."

With a smile he squeezed Katria's hand and left them to wander the state room a bit, searching. He had another he needed to speak with before their plans continued. Where was the man? Spotting Lazarenko along a far wall, Anatoli headed toward the unsuspecting man.

He needed to tip off the Third Section about the Radoffs.

Chapter Twenty

March 6, 1855
Georgian Calendar

SERGEY RADOFF waited as the Third Section secret police rifled through his house. Sipping a rather fine Spanish port, he continued to read Pushkin as they tore through his papers and thumbed through every book. At the moment, the poet's subversive writings appealed to him.

He wasn't worried. There was nothing in this house for them to find. Damn Alexey Orlov! If the man hadn't returned to St. Petersburg for Nicholas's funeral, he could have continued on. Damn Nikolai Orlov, too, and his family ties.

Still, there was nothing here. All papers remotely tying him to Peter's supposed discoveries were destroyed along with Peter and Constantine Markova. Viktor was mumbling about Katria resisting the engagement to Pavel, but Sergey was confident that, too, could be overcome.

A loud crash echoed through the hall. Sergey winced. "Don't let that be the Louis XIV vase," he snapped to no one in particular.

Forcing himself not to rise and see for himself, not to give the Third Section anything to use against him, he read the same paragraph again.

Alexey Orlov and Lazarenko walked by, the latter limping as he held his thigh. Sergey paid them no mind, but the very fact that Alexey had involved himself in this search had him setting aside *Skupoy rytsar*, *The Miserly Knight*, and rising. They entered the music room, scanning the little-used furniture as if they searched for something specific.

"You won't find anything worth breaking here," Sergey said, adjusting his cuffs. "It's only used when we entertain on a large scale."

Alexey dismissed him with an impatient wave. Gritting his teeth, Sergey said nothing. Alexey had the ultimate trust of Nicholas. Just because that man now lay dead did not mean Alexander II wouldn't listen to him.

"Search the room," Alexey commanded his men. To Lazarenko he said, "Even the fireplace."

Unease settled in Sergey's belly. *The fireplace?* Lazarenko ran his hands over the outside of it along the marble face. When he stuck his head inside, Sergey had a feeling he was being set up. Katria had wandered the house unescorted mere days ago.

But the other man, now covered in soot, emerged empty-handed.

"See?" Sergey asked, triumphant. "Nothing. Enough of this, Count Orlov. What revenge are you exacting?"

"No revenge, Count Radoff," Alexey said smoothly. "We are merely investigating allegations against you."

Lazarenko rejoined Alexey and handed him a paper. "I found this, sir."

Sergey didn't move. Almost simultaneously, as Alexey read the paper, another Third Section man entered. "Sir!" he called, and handed the count a small bottle. Alexey held it up to the light.

"Take him into custody," Alexey ordered. "Keep it discreet."

Sergey protested, but it was no use. He struggled against the hands binding him, and spat on Alexey. "This is your doing!"

Calmly pulling out a handkerchief and wiping his face, Alexey asked, "Where's your son, Radoff?"

Snarling, Sergey said nothing. Alexey gestured to have him removed like a rabid dog, and the Third Section officers prepared to haul him out of his own house.

"Take him to my special rooms in the Palace," Alexey commanded. "I'll meet with the tsar and present the evidence myself."

****

Pavel watched the black-clad Third Section drag his father out of the house. Sergey, the bastard, looked regal even now when he had been caught—no, *arrested*—by the tsar's secret police. Whatever Sergey was involved with, Pavel didn't want it spilling onto him.

Before they saw him, he turned and walked back the way he'd come.

Elizabetta's warm body beckoned him. Despite the fact he just left her, and the unending vodka she supplied, Pavel had nowhere else to go. Hunching deeper into his coat, he walked faster. It was that plot against the Orlovs that finally caught up with Sergey. Once Alexey returned from wherever in hell he was, it was a matter of time before the head of the Third Section cleared his nephew's name.

Rounding a corner, the stench of urine and rotten food hit him. God, he hated this section of St. Petersburg. If the women weren't so willing, he'd—

Horse's hooves pounded behind him. Turning, he saw a well-dressed gentleman on horseback, his face covered by heavy winter garb. There was something familiar about the scene, about the man. Hurrying down the alleyway, toward the brothel, Pavel couldn't shake the horse. The rider was relentless.

Glancing over his shoulder, Pavel saw the rider dismount, walking toward him with a revolver aimed steadily at his chest. The scene was eerily familiar and he ran. Heavy footsteps, muffled by the snow, chased after him.

Over his shoulder, he saw his pursuer remove the scarf from his face. Nikolai. Skidding to a halt, Pavel turned and confronted him.

"Orlov, you son of a bitch," Pavel screamed. "What have you done? You used your uncle to frame my father for what crime?"

"There are so many," Orlov retorted. Then, to his surprise, the other man tossed his gun into the snow, dropping the scarf next to it. "Let's see if you can fight, you treasonous bastard."

Pavel looked about the ground for something to use for leverage: a pipe, a hunk of wood. Nikolai seemed not to care, and steadily advanced on him. There was nothing; the peasants had rummaged the streets for firewood and snowdrifts covered everything else but a few bits of trash.

Frustrated, he grabbed a handful of snow and threw it at Nikolai. The other man grinned, an evil grin that promised retribution.

Tired of this, tired of being faced down by Nikolai, he walked forward. "Accept your losses, Orlov. Katria is mine. And I'll use her as I see fit."

He swung at the taller man's face, but Orlov blocked the attempt. As Pavel brought up his other arm, Orlov hit back. He didn't miss. The brawl was vicious, and Pavel, who didn't know any other way to fight but dirty, found himself on the losing end. No matter how he lashed out, how many times he kicked the other man, Orlov landed more blows.

Pavel's nose was bloodied, several ribs had cracked despite the heavy clothing he wore, and he feared his jaw was broken.

Orlov's gloved hand caught his head, and Pavel, too weak to resist, saw the brick wall closing in.

"She would have enjoyed spreading her legs for me."

The last thing Pavel thought was that this was one problem his father couldn't fix. Then his head smashed against the wall and pain exploded around him. He dimly felt himself fall to the ground, the cold of the snow barely registering against his cheek.

Nikolai looked down at Pavel's dead body. His death did little to alleviate the rage he carried toward the other man. It wasn't because of his role, whatever it may have been, in Peter's death. It was his threat to Katria.

If it had been only against Peter, Nikolai wondered if he'd have tracked Pavel's movements so closely. Yes. But he suspected he'd have given the information to Alexey, filtered it through Anatoli.

The fact the other man touched Katria, threatened her life, her health—Nikolai turned, gathering his scarf and gun.

She'd be safe now.

****

Nikolai patiently waited as Alexey Orlov signed several papers. He smiled at Lazarenko as the other man eyed him warily.

"Your return is timely, Uncle," he said the moment they were alone.

"So it seems. I understand you rendered assistance to the Third Section while I was away."

Grinning innocuously, Nikolai shrugged. "I don't know what you mean." Changing the subject he said, "Have you discovered Pavel Radoff's whereabouts?"

Alexey's eyes narrowed, but Nikolai looked on with polite interest. "No, not as yet. We're scouring the city for him. He may have information of his father's activities."

"Hmm," Nikolai said. "I doubt that. Have you checked all the brothels in the city's limits? I'm certain he's cowering under a whore's bed. Or the Neva—I understand it's quite dangerous." Alexey nodded and Nikolai tugged on his gloves and retrieved his walking stick. "I wouldn't worry, Uncle. I don't think he'll be a problem any longer."

"I had that feeling, Nikolai." Alexey stood and before Nikolai could open the door said, "I'd appreciate you leaving my officers alone. I can't afford to lose any more."

Laughing, Nikolai agreed. "You should hire more trustworthy spies then, Uncle." He yanked open the door, then paused. "But the way, how is Lazarenko's leg?"

Alexey looked confused, then suspicious. Whistling as he left the offices on the lower levels of the Winter Palace, Nikolai offered a jaunty wave at Lazarenko. The other man scowled.

****

March 9, 1855
Georgian Calendar

"The engagement between Radoff and Katria is off."

Katria noticed Viktor's voice was pleased as he told another group of courtiers the happy news. Well, she was happy; she couldn't say how he truly felt about it, however joyfully he played it to the court. Always the consummate viper. She smiled at her analogy and mused that Nikolai would laugh.

"Pavel treated my daughter poorly," Viktor continued. "And with Nikolai Orlov's name now unblemished, I've decided to allow the children to marry. Orlov has proved himself a fine man and a wonderful addition to our family."

Katria heard a couple of titters, saw Princess Ulensky—who seemed to be everywhere she was these days—glance at her with a knowing smile, and set off to find Nikolai. She spotted Anatoli first.

"A moment, Katria?"

"Of course, Uncle."

He drew her to one side, waving off those with whom he'd been speaking. "Sergey Radoff has been found guilty by the Third Section and the tsar. He's accused of murdering Tsar Nicholas I, and of treasonous acts against our beloved Russia."

Katria suppressed her smirk of satisfaction.

"You may be assured," Anatoli continued with a slight grin, "he'll not darken our doorstep again."

Nodding, she said, "Thank you, Uncle. I'll be sure to relay that to Constantine, who is much improved." Squeezing his hand, she said sincerely, "Thank you." Kissing him on both cheeks, she turned to find Nikolai.

She caught his attention and tilted her head toward an empty salon. When he joined her scant moments later, she rushed into his arms.

"It's over."

His body was warm and hard against hers, his mouth hungry as he kissed her. "Until the next time the vipers intend to strike," he said into her neck. "But then it won't matter." He returned to her mouth.

"No?" she asked, backing him against the door. She wanted to laugh at him for using her viper analogy, but his mouth was distracting. She'd tell him later, after he sated the craving he'd sparked within her. "You're right. It won't."

He laughed, picking her up and pressing her to the wall. Katria wrapped her arms around him and whispered against his lips, "Take me home, Nikolai. Make love to me."

THE END

Author's Note

IN RUSSIA, both past and present, one addresses even a close acquaintance with both first name and patronymic. A patronymic is personal name based on the name of one's father, grandfather or an even earlier male ancestor. In this case, it denotes ancestry: *son of Ivan* or *daughter of Ivan*.

For instance, Katria Viktorevna Markova would always be referred to as Katria Viktorevna by everyone but her immediate family (parents, siblings, favorite uncle) and closest friends (Anna Pietrovena Tiomkin in the story). *Katria daughter of Victor; Anna daughter of Pietro.*

For simplicity's sake, I introduced everyone using their entire name: Katria Viktorevna; Nikolai Andreiovich; Anatoli Mikhailivitch; Sergey Ivanovich; Pavel Sergeivich…etc., then dropped the patronymic.

Until the revolution in 1917, Russia didn't use the same calendar as the Western world. It was called the Old Style. I changed the dates to reflect the Western dates.

Also unique to Russia were the classifications of nobility. There were three levels of nobility, baron/baroness, count/countess, prince/princess. Russia is an autocratic society, so the tsar had ultimate control over who became which noble, when, and for what reason. Royalty, the tsar's extended family, were Grand—Grand Dukes, Grand Princesses.

His immediate family were also Grand: Grand Duchess Anastasia, for instance; his male heirs were all titled Grand Dukes, with his direct male heir *Tsesarevich*.

I tried not to delve too deeply into this, because of the confusion surrounding it.

The Orlovs were a real family, mostly known for deposing Peter III and bringing Catherine II to the throne. But their descendants remained loyal to the Romanov family afterwards. Catherine elevated the family to counts, Alexander III to princes. I created a fictitious branch of this famous family. Alexey Fyodorovich Orlov was a real diplomat and head of the Third Section.

The Third Section is the name of the Tsarist secret police. It's the third department of the tsar's chancellery: First Section: Majestic Decrees and Orders; Second Section: Codification of Imperial Legislation; Third Section: Secret Police, Fourth Section: Charities for the Dowager Empress Maria Fedorovna, and so on. Alexey answered directly to the tsar; in this case Nicholas I. According to *KGB: The Inside Story of its Intelligence Operations from Lenin to Gorbachev* by Christopher Andrew and Oleg Gordievsky, the Third Section was created in 1825 and included only sixteen investigators. In 1855, that number increased to forty, but in 1880 it was replaced by Okhrana.